
★

I tried to organize the information I'd gathered on Harry. The few facts were all negative—he wasn't painting, he wasn't drinking, he wasn't responsible for Mary's death—and I soon grew discouraged. I mentally shifted my field of view, reviewing instead the thin file on my other mystery, Diana Lord. She had recently changed her mind about getting married. She had money. She could mysteriously enter locked rooms. She was interested in death—too interested, if Father Peter's insight was correct. She was fascinated by the story of Brigid Kelly. She swam every night in the lake in which Brigid had drowned.

My damp shirt suddenly felt cool against my back. I was reminded of the two warnings I had received regarding Diana, Shelly's maternal advice that she was troubled and Peter's blunt judgment that I was out of my league.

★

"It's hard to find a place to take a break as each page flows from one scene to another..."
—Ocala Star-Banner

Terence Faherty

Live To Regret

WORLDWIDE.®

TORONTO • NEW YORK • LONDON
AMSTERDAM • PARIS • SYDNEY • HAMBURG
STOCKHOLM • ATHENS • TOKYO • MILAN
MADRID • WARSAW • BUDAPEST • AUCKLAND

LIVE TO REGRET

A Worldwide Mystery/October 1995

First published by St. Martin's Press, Incorporated.

ISBN 0-373-26180-2

Quotations from "Out of the Cradle Endlessly Rocking" by Walt Whitman conform to the version contained in the ninth edition of *Leaves of Grass*, the "deathbed" edition of 1892.

Printed in U.S.A.

For my parents

A FUNERAL

MARY WAS DEAD; that much was certain. There would have been nothing remarkable about what happened afterward if that terrible statement were not true. Mary Ohlman, my friend and onetime love, was dead, killed in an automobile accident, and I had come to say good-bye to her on a hard, gray February morning.

I sat in the back of a tiny, wooden church that groaned and creaked with the shifting of the crowd like a ship in a heavy sea. We were listening to the words of an aged priest who, for once, had actually known the person whose life he was summing up. Mary had been a person worth knowing, and the priest struggled to convey that. But instead of isolating the one thing that had made her special, he piled up clichés in an improbable, impersonal monument. She was a giving person. She never met a stranger. She had a smile for everyone. I became impatient with this and began to word my own silent rebuttal. She was good, I wanted to tell the dark, bent gathering. That was the rare, unlikely fact of it. Yes, she was a strong friend, a good mother, a loving wife. She was accomplished and gifted and bright. But what we were missing now was something more than all those things and something simpler. She was good, and she expected goodness from the people she met, a ridiculous long shot that always seemed to come in for her. She believed

that the world around her had goodness as its basis
and its underlying truth. She'd died believing that, an
uncommon feat.

In the end, the priest succeeded without my help and
in spite of himself. His own obvious grief and confu-
sion conveyed a meaning too heavy for his words to
bear.

I took my place at the end of Mary's funeral procession, conscious of my grandmother's superstition
that the last in line would be the next to die. It was a
long line of cars, out of all proportion to the short
distance to be covered. Mary was halfway to her grave
before my tired wheels had begun to roll. The cemetery was on a hillside exposed to the winter wind.
Many of the mourners stayed in their cars, and the
group by the open grave crowded tightly together. I
was in no mood for even that small interaction. I
walked up the hill above the gathering and watched
from the thin shadow of a cedar tree and the company of older, quieter graves.

The old priest was speaking again, but his words
were whipped away by the same north wind that tore
at his vestments. I supplied my own text. My theme
was "she is gone." During her funeral mass and now
as I watched the priest sprinkling holy water on the
wind, I was struck by the contradiction between the
stated message of the service and its hidden lesson. For
while the words conveyed the Christian consolation
that Mary lived on, that she was now in a better world
where we would someday join her, the service seemed
designed to help us accept the opposite hard truth:
Mary was dead, she was gone, she was lost to us forever. Maybe it was just the unhappy time of year
working on me. There was no comfort in the thought

of Mary lying in that frozen ground, no beauty in the gray, windswept ceremony.

I watched as the mourners filed slowly past the grave before they hurried off to their warm cars. Then Mary's family placed their flowers on the casket and withdrew. I remained behind as the procession wound back down the hill, watching two workmen in muddy overalls begin the task of covering the grave. A long good-bye was justified, I told myself. It was unlikely that my wanderings would bring me to this cold hillside again.

ONE

It was July 1986. I was on stakeout duty in Spring Lake, a small resort town on the New Jersey shore, observing the activities of Harry Ohlman, my old college friend and former employer. Harry was in Spring Lake recuperating from injuries he'd suffered in the automobile accident in which his wife, Mary, had died. That was his story anyway. My job was to find out what he was really up to. My name, incidentally, is Owen Keane.

I had been in Spring Lake only a week, but I had already identified Harry's routine, what little there was. By this particular morning, a Tuesday, I was settled enough in my own routine to wake before my alarm clock went off. That was just as well. My early risings were as unpopular with my fellow boarders as Harry's were with me. Ten minutes later, I was dressed in orange running shorts, a mesh shirt, running shoes with bright green laces, and a matching cap. I added bulky headphones with a built-in radio and, finally, the standard disguise of that time, dark sunglasses with black plastic frames. I caught sight of myself in the mirror over my dresser and thought of how Mary would have laughed to see me in my getup, playing detective again. I had to put the image of Mary out of my head as quickly as it had come, or I would have sunk back down on the edge of the bed with my head in my hands and done nothing. Instead, I went down three flights of creaking stairs and let myself out into the misty street.

I set out for the lake that separated my rented room from Harry's rented cottage. By degrees, I became aware of the morning. I shivered in the damp coolness. I noted the heavy dew on the browned-out lawns. I heard for the first time that day the sound I'd heard every day for the past week, the soft working of the ocean. Spring Lake was a turn-of-the-century shore resort that had survived, tattered but largely unchanged, into the 1980s. A new generation had recently discovered it, and the result was something of a renaissance. The rambling Italianate three-story where I rented my room had once been a guest house and was now a bed and breakfast. It was currently being repainted an authentic olive green with dark red trim. The eccentric Victorian homes I passed on my walk to the lake were one by one undergoing the same rebirth.

At the center of the town lay the lake that had given the place its name and its reason for being, a small freshwater lake a quarter mile from the ocean. On that particular morning, the lake was also the center of the light fog that had spread out through the town's broad streets. The mist made the lake banks ill-defined and created the illusion that the wooden footbridge that crossed the lake at its narrow waist was floating in midair. As I approached the lake, I saw on its far bank St. Brigid's Church, a darker gray mass in the gray air. Too small to be the basilica its designer had imitated and too dense with granite and marble to be a small-town church, it made me think that morning of a mausoleum monstrously grown. I shivered a second time.

I took up my post on the opposite side of the lake from Harry's cottage, under a large maple tree next to the sign that listed the various things—swimming, boating, fishing—you couldn't do in the lake. There I began, self-consciously, to do whatever stretching exercises I could recall from high school track practices. It wasn't very long before I heard the hollow pounding of Harry's footsteps on the bridge. The sound seemed too loud by far in the morning stillness, like a car horn blaring or a dog barking. I glanced up briefly to confirm that it was Harry and then went back to my exercises. I was using Edgar Allan Poe's formula for hiding something, which is to make the hidden thing—in this case, myself—as conspicuous as possible. That was the logic behind my gaudy outfit. Not only were the neon clothes out of character for me, and therefore a disguise, they made it certain that Harry would notice me every morning, so I would eventually disappear into the scenery.

That was my plan, but something peculiar about Harry made me suspect that my scheme was so much wasted brilliance. I'd noticed that on his morning walks Harry strode along with his head erect and his eyes straight before him, apparently oblivious to the town and the people around him. I had the feeling that I could have followed a few steps behind him in my pajamas and he would never have seen me. I had noticed something else I couldn't explain, something I didn't like. As he marched along, Harry smiled broadly. A smile was the wrong expression for a recent widower who, I had been assured, was wasting away from grief.

Harry passed within fifty yards of me as he climbed up the bank from the bridge to the street. He never took his eyes from the path before him. He was wearing a plain white tee shirt and gray sweat pants, and his dark hair was longer than he'd worn it in years. He headed for Durbin Street, the shortest route between his cottage and the beach. I gave Harry a few minutes' head start, and then jogged up Durbin after him. There was no danger of my overtaking him. Harry strode ahead like a man leading a parade, his chest thrown out, his hands raised like a boxer's, his arms swinging aggressively. I was breathing faster before we'd gone a block. We both stuck to the street. The sidewalks on either side of us were as old as the houses we passed, and treacherous. They'd been cracked and shoved up like tiny mountain ranges by the sycamore trees that lined the road. These trees were everywhere in Spring Lake, lumpy and deformed from years of pruning. That morning they made me think of lines of Spring Lake retirees frozen in their daily march to the beach.

The ocean first appeared as a blinding light at the end of the street, a Hollywood-style symbol of salvation created by the rising sun reflecting from a thousand waves. Harry turned his back to the light and strode backward down the street. This maneuver took me by surprise, and for a panicked second I thought of dropping to retie a shoe or dodging behind the nearest sycamore. In the end, I did the correct thing, which was to jog along indifferently. Harry showed no signs of noticing me. The earlier coolness was just a memory now, along with the gray mist. I could feel the heat of the sun on my face, and I noted Harry pulling at the front of his shirt before he swung around again to face his line of march.

Harry crossed the beach road, Ocean Avenue, and
headed south on the elevated boardwalk. I crossed the
street and the boardwalk and descended the sandy
concrete steps to the beach before heading south myself. At once, I lost the illusion of isolation that the fog
and the early hour had created. Ahead of me, an older
couple wearing windbreakers and shapeless hats
leaned toward one another as they walked. To their
left, near the glittering ocean, a single figure wandered among the gulls, poking at the morning seaweed with a stick. This person was old, too, her steps
an uncertain shuffle across the sand. The town's
younger element was up on the boardwalk with Harry.
Well-tanned and dressed in outfits that made my disguise look sedate, they jogged and walked and ran
singly and in pairs, eyeing one another openly and ex-
changing greetings as they passed. Harry, as far as I
could tell, took no part in this.

My mind wandered as I padded along at the water's edge, attracted first to the patterns formed by
spent waves as the last bubbling foam disappeared into
the firm sand and then by the darting play of tiny birds
who chased the retreating waves on stiff stilt legs in
search of something they never seemed to find. Finally, I turned to the question I'd asked myself every
day for the past week. What was I doing in Spring
Lake? I knew the simple answer. I was watching over
Harry Ohlman, whose extended absence from home
and routine had begun to worry his family. I also knew
that the simple answer was wrong, that there was more
going on than it could explain. As usual, I had begun
to compile my own agenda, different from my clients'. At the top of my list was another question. Why
was Harry smiling?

I looked for Harry in the light boardwalk traffic and noted that he had begun to favor his right leg, the one that had been badly broken in the accident. I'd noticed on previous walks Harry's tendency to overdo it. He seemed determined to ignore the weakness in his leg, as though by ignoring it he could make it go away. The limping usually signaled a turn toward home, but this morning Harry pushed stubbornly onward. He went half a mile further than we'd ever gone before, all the way to the Waterbury Hotel, the unofficial southern boundary of the town. I marveled at the old landmark, whose classical façade masked a full block of shantytown wings and additions. In a town that was restoring itself and taking pride in its Victorian roots, the Waterbury seemed to stand as a memorial to the years of slow decline. It looked to me to be a symbol of the past in general: a jumble of conflicting intentions that could never be put right, only complicated endlessly.

Harry left the boardwalk at Waterbury Street and headed west. Gambling that he would follow a straight line back to the lake, I climbed onto the boardwalk and continued south for a block at my top speed. Then I turned right onto Cleveland, which paralleled Waterbury. When I reached the first cross street, which had the poetic name of Murtland, I looked across toward Waterbury and caught sight of Harry. His limp was pronounced now. His weak leg had forced him from his long, aggressive stride to a normal walk. I gratefully slowed to a walk myself, maintaining my parallel course on Cleveland. I would arrive at the lake just after Harry, if I was careful to match my pace to his.

I used the quiet time to consider the problem of
Harry's smile and my reaction to it. Seeing that innocent expression had somehow brought into focus all
the anger and resentment I'd been living with since
Mary's death. Focused it and directed it at the smiler,
Harry. As his friend, I should have been grateful for
any sign that he was recovering from his loss. Instead, I was angry. Why? It was another question I
couldn't answer yet, another one for my personal research list.

Cleveland ended at Lake Shore Drive, a road that
went nowhere but around and around Spring Lake.
There was no sign of Harry. I knew he hadn't gotten
ahead of me. From where I stood, I could see all the
way across the lake to the door of his cottage. I sat
down on a curb at the base of yet another misshapen
sycamore and waited. From its shade, I watched a
solitary runner circling the lake, matching stride for
stride his reflection in the smooth water. To my left,
two early worshippers climbed the steps of St. Brigid's. The church had lost its sepulcher look and now
sat placidly in the full sun. Traffic around the lake had
picked up, a reminder that not everyone here was va-
cationing or retired. I remembered myself that I was a
member of that working group and struggled to my
feet.

Harry finally appeared at the end of Waterbury. He
was limping badly now. His hair was pasted down with
sweat, and his tee shirt was pink where it had stuck to
his back. The smile that had so offended me was gone,
and with it went a small part of my anger. I watched
with increasing concern as Harry hobbled along the
lake's grassy bank to the footbridge. Before he reached
the bridge, he gave up his poor imitation of a normal

stride and began to hop on his good left leg with only a token steadying from his right. I started to jog after Harry, the job of learning his secret suddenly less involving than his struggle to get back to his cottage.

I checked my pace when Harry reached the footbridge. He stopped to rest for a moment before starting across, leaning with both arms on the railing and staring down into the water. I watched him from beneath the same maple tree where I'd done my elaborate warm-up half an hour earlier. Harry then began to move cautiously across the bridge, using the same hopping step and supporting himself on the railing with both hands. As he limped up the bank on the far side, I sat down again in the cool grass.

My relaxation was premature. Harry fell while trying to clear his last hurdle, the curb at his own front walk. I got up and started to run across to him. Harry was back on his feet quickly, but he fell a second time before I'd reached the footbridge. Without thinking it through, I had decided to drop my surveillance and help my friend. The bad feeling that I'd let build up like a wall between us was gone for a moment. It came back in a rush as Harry, in his pain, began to call out the name of his dead wife.

I stopped in my tracks, halfway across the bridge, and watched Harry crawl back into his cottage.

TWO

HARRY'S PART OF the story had really begun two weeks earlier when I received a letter that made me think of detective stories I'd read as a boy. I was living in Red Bank then, a town of about ten thousand people in the corner of New Jersey that juts out from under New York City to meet the sea. I was helping an old friend of mine, Brother Stephen Murawski, who ran a retreat house for high school kids during his summer breaks from teaching. He and I met at another such retreat years before and had knocked heads, but our relationship had since mellowed, Stephen having a weakness for black sheep that caused him endless trouble. I was between jobs at the time the letter found me, and that coincidence also reminded me of long-ago mystery stories. The detective was always between jobs when the big case arrived.

The return address on the envelope contained the name of a New York law firm: Ohlman, Pulsifer, and Hurst. When I worked there five years before, it had been Ohlman, Ohlman, and Pulsifer, the first name referring to Harry's father, now retired. I had been a researcher for the firm, until the day I decided that my own researches were more important to me. Since that time, I had been a number of things, all the while carefully avoiding the prosperity that most of the country was enjoying. I had stumbled across some interesting cases, though, and even solved one or two of them. I had no complaints on that score.

Inside the envelope was a plane ticket and a short letter typed on the firm's letterhead. The letter was from the man whose name had been removed from the shingle, Harold Ohlman, Sr., and it read:

Dear Mr. Keane:
Please use the enclosed ticket to visit me at Masthead Farm on Tuesday the eighth. Forgive the short notice. Consider it a reflection of the extreme urgency of the request. You will be met at the airport.

The signature at the bottom was followed by the initials LK. I recognized the initials as those of Ms. Kiefner, Harry's secretary and an old nemesis of mine. The ticket was a round trip from Newark to Hyannis on Cape Cod via an airline I'd never heard of.

I began to make deductions about the letter, in the classic detective style. Almost all my guesses were wrong, in the classic Keane style. I thought, for example, that Mr. Ohlman had some discreet research project that needed my special talents. Harry had probably recommended me, I decided. That would account for Ms. Kiefner's participation. Even though we had seen each other only occasionally since I'd left his firm and not at all since I'd visited him in the hospital after Mary's funeral, it was natural to think of Harry looking out for me. We'd been friends since college, and, although we were the same age, Harry had always assumed toward me the role of an older brother saddled with an irresponsible, impractical sibling.

I'd been laid up emotionally since Mary's death, observing the parade of lengthening days without interest or enthusiasm. I saw Mr. Ohlman's letter as a possible diversion from my dark thoughts. I don't think that under any circumstances I could have resisted a mysterious invitation with an airline ticket attached. On that particular morning, as I stood holding the letter with one hand while I stirred a gallon of soup with the other, the decision required no effort at all.

I was afraid that Brother Stephen would complain about his cook resigning on short notice. Instead, he echoed my own vague hopes. "Do you good," he said in his north Jersey gangster voice. "You've been mooning around all summer."

On Tuesday morning I dressed in my best suit and drove to Newark International where I handed myself over to a small commuter airline for the hour-long flight to Hyannis. Every seat in the tiny twin-engine plane was taken, which enabled me to add claustrophobia to my normal preflight uneasiness. As it turned out, the trip was smooth and uneventful, except for the sight of a great deal of water passing under the wings.

We landed at Barnstable Municipal Airport, where, I had been told, I would be met. I entered the tiny terminal looking for Mr. Ohlman or someone holding up a sign with my name on it. I saw only one unattached person. He was standing in the center of the single room shared by a ticket counter, a passenger lounge, and the baggage claim desk. He wore a khaki-colored cap with a long bill that stuck up at an angle like the flag on a mailbox. The sleeves of his gray shirt were rolled up past his elbows, and the legs of his baggy tan pants ended in similar rolls that lay across the tops of his shoes. I guessed his age at fifty. He was tanned to a dark red, and his light blue eyes found me as soon as I came through the door.

"I'm Ralph," the man said as I stepped up to him. "The car's outside."

Ralph was not happy with me for some reason. Maybe he had expected me to be carrying a sign with his name on it. As he led me outside to a huge Olds-mobile station wagon, his pointed silence revived the uneasiness I'd felt during the flight. It occurred to me for the first time that this little adventure of mine might have been a bad idea.

I had made weekend trips to Cape Cod during my college days at Boston, but seeing it again still sur-prised me. I was more used to the southern New Jer-sey shore, where the topography changed to flat, sandy pine forests forty miles or more from the ocean. On our family drives to the beach, those miles of roadside edged in sand had exaggerated the anticipa-tion, creating the agonizing impression that we were always almost there. The area around Orleans on the Cape created the opposite false impression. Ralph and I drove over small hills, past neat white houses and tiny antique barns that seem too like New England to be real. The trees were still deciduous, and the yards were green and ordinary. Then suddenly, at the top of yet another hillock, I saw the ocean.

Masthead Farm, the Ohlmans' retirement prop-erty, sat on the top of that last grassy hill, from which the dark blue of the ocean was just visible beneath a hazy sky. The name of the farm, an obvious reference to the view, appeared on a freshly painted sign large enough to grace a country inn. The house itself was unpretentious and very like its neighbors, except that it was gray instead of white. It was actually several buildings joined, or rather a house that had been added onto several times. The effect was not rambling or haphazard. The additions, though smaller in size, retained the stolid proportions and clapboard siding of the original house. The result was something unified and oddly natural looking, like an outcropping of gray stone exposed at the top of the hill.

Ralph parked the station wagon at the head of the gravel drive without breaking his silence. I wondered as I climbed out if I would have to find my own way into the house. Mr. Harold Ohlman ended the suspense by appearing at a screened doorway.

"Owen," he said. "It was good of you to come. How was your flight? Come in."

He led me along a corridor that rose and dropped and jogged left and right as it passed through the additions and into the main part of the house. All the while, my host chatted away happily. I was reminded of an old office assessment of Harry's father: he was professionally discreet but privately delighted in gossip.

"You last worked for us on the Carteret Federal Bank business," he said without pausing for me to confirm it. "You've heard about the bank, I suppose."

"No," I said.

"It's gone. Bought up by First Empire. Swallowed up in a gulp and gone. These takeovers unsettle me. It's the work of a lifetime building up a business. Sometimes several lifetimes as they're passed from one generation to the next. Then overnight, they're gone. Of course, the Carteret family wasn't affected by the loss of the bank. The last Carteret, Robert, died in 1984. Did you know that?"

"Yes," I said. "I went to his funeral."

Mr. Ohlman turned to read my expression. When he had determined that I was serious, he nodded his head and filed that bit of information away.

We had arrived in a large room whose pine paneling shone in the late morning sunlight. There were bookcases crowded with legal volumes on either side of a stone fireplace. Above its mantel hung a print of Boston's Faneuil Hall. It reminded me that Mr. Ohlman had not been a New York lawyer by choice, but only because it had been decreed by his family's original Boston firm.

Mr. Ohlman settled lightly on the edge of a small desk that sat at an angle across one corner of the room. He pointed to a barrel-back chair that looked more comfortable than it turned out to be.

"So," he said after I had seated myself. "How are you doing, son?"

The familiar form of address set me on my guard, as it presumed a closer relationship than he and I had ever enjoyed. Mr. Ohlman, on the other hand, looked perfectly relaxed. Despite the warmth of the day, he wore a long-sleeve, plaid shirt buttoned to the neck and well-pressed corduroy trousers. His gray hair was close-cut and parted high on one side of his head in a dated style. He was a short, slight man, unlike his son, and his small stature kept the fact that he was now looking down at me from being more than slightly irritating.

"I'm doing fine," I said.

"Careerwise, I mean."

"That's fine, too."

"Really? You'll forgive me for observing this, Owen, but the store that sold you that suit probably had a lawn and garden department." He paused to smile at his own joke. "How many jobs have you had since you left the firm?"

"A number," I said.

"A nice round number, from what I've been able to learn."

"I take what interests me," I said.

I had either colored as I said it or else my tone had conveyed my embarrassment. Mr. Ohlman held up one hand in a conciliatory gesture. "I'm not trying to pry," he said. "I'm working my way up to a proposition. A mutually beneficial one. I want you to take on a job for me. You would be back on the payroll of the firm and all your expenses would be paid. Nothing permanent, you understand, but that's probably to your liking."

"What's the assignment?" I asked.

Mr. Ohlman stared at me for a second as though he still hadn't made up his mind to share the secret. Then he said: "I want you to look after Harry."

"I don't understand."

"Neither do I," Mr. Ohlman replied. "That's the problem. I don't understand why he's not bouncing back. That sounds too trite to describe my son's situation, but that's the case. He's not bouncing back. Not healing."

"I take it you're not referring to his broken leg," I said.

"No," Mr. Ohlman said. "The problem isn't physical healing. He's doing fine in that respect. The pins are out of his leg. He's off his crutches. No, I was referring to his spirit. Harry's not bouncing back from his loss."

My expression must have conveyed my objection to that, because Mr. Ohlman hurried to answer it. "I know losing Mary was a tremendous blow," he said, turning his head to stare into the empty fireplace. "It was for all of us. Mother and I thought of Mary as our own daughter. We loved her. Everybody did." He eyed me obliquely for a moment, looking for another reaction that he could file away. When I didn't oblige him, he turned to face me. "A person recovers from a blow like that or fails to. Harry is not recovering."

"What exactly is he doing?" I asked.

"I don't know that either. I mean I don't know what he's really doing. I know he's staying at the Jersey shore, alone, in a house with no telephone. We invited him here, of course, but he wouldn't come. He told me he wanted to paint."

"He used to paint well," I said. "He often spoke of getting away and doing it again."

"Yes," Mr. Ohlman said. "That was always his excuse when he didn't want to be working on something serious. I think it's only an excuse now, something to let him escape his responsibilities."

"Are you referring to the firm or to Amanda?" I asked. Amanda was Harry's daughter, who would be five in a month or so.

"I was referring to the firm *and* Amanda." Mr. Ohlman's relaxed grace disappeared, and he leaned stiffly toward me. "I'll not apologize for being concerned with the business I built myself. It's my legacy to Harry. It's his security and Amanda's."

"Where is she?" I asked.

"Here," he said, gesturing vaguely over his shoulder toward the bright windows. "Helping her grandmother garden. She's doing well, bless her. There's a great deal of strength in that child. But she needs her father."

"He would need her if he were doing anything like getting on with his life," I said, thinking aloud.

"Exactly," Mr. Ohlman said. "You can see now why I'm asking for your help. We must find out what Harry's up to."

"I'm not a private investigator," I said. "That's what you need."

"I need you, Owen. You're uniquely qualified to handle this. You were Harry's roommate in college. You know him. You knew Mary. No one I could hire would have your insight. And there are other things to recommend you. Details of your background." I didn't acknowledge that reference, so he spelled it out for me. "You once studied for the priesthood, I believe."

"What has that got to do with Harry?"

"I believe Harry is undergoing a spiritual crisis. That's something else no private investigator could deal with. I suspect that Harry is drinking heavily, and I'm afraid he may be doing something worse."

"Drugs?" I asked.

Mr. Ohlman lowered his voice without taking his eyes from mine. "That would explain why he had hidden himself away," he said.

The possibility gave the knot that had been forming in my stomach a sharp twist. I suddenly wanted to be out of that room, out of that house, and far away from the Ohlmans. It was a reaction I didn't fully understand, in part an irrational anger at the injustice of

Mary's death, in part the feeling that I hadn't "bounced back" from it myself, that it was unfair to ask me to hold Harry's hand or anyone else's.

While I thought seriously about walking back to Red Bank, Mr. Ohlman described how the firm would back me in my inquiries, giving me an "official status" and providing any resources I needed. He must have considered the discussion of salary to be indelicate, because he glossed over it, and he looked positively embarrassed as he handed me a credit card. My name was already embossed on its golden plastic.

I handed the card back to him. "I'm sorry," I began. "I'm too close to this situation to be any good to you or to Harry."

That was as far as I got. Mrs. Ohlman entered the room, as if on cue. "Owen," she said. "I'm so glad you're going to help us."

I stood up. As advertised, she was dressed for gardening in an untucked cotton work shirt and jeans. She wiped her hands on a short canvas apron before shaking mine.

"Owen hasn't made up his mind just yet," Mr. Ohlman said. "He wants to think it over."

"You're staying for lunch, of course," Mrs. Ohlman said to me. "Amanda's been looking forward to it."

"Yes," I said. "I'd like that." I didn't look over at Mr. Ohlman, afraid I'd find him smiling at his cleverness.

"Good," Mrs. Ohlman said. "Come out and see her now." She took me by the hand and led me back along the crooked corridor and out into the backyard. She was a tall woman, only slightly settled with age. In addition to his height, Harry had inherited from her his artistic leanings. According to Harry, his mother's great sadness had been never finding the right medium for her own creativity. It might have been that failure that gave her the distant, unfocused quality I noted on our infrequent meetings. She was a sweet person despite her quiet detachment, and I liked her.

As we walked single file along a narrow, climbing, flagstone path, Mrs. Ohlman suddenly addressed me as though she and I had been discussing Harry's mystery for hours. "There's one thing I've been thinking about," she said. "It's a poem."

"A poem?"

"Yes. I can't remember the title or the poet, isn't that silly? It's about a bird and the ocean."

"A bird," I repeated.

"And the ocean," Mrs. Ohlman said patiently. "Every time I think of poor Harry, I feel an echo of that poem. It's just there," she added, indicating a point in the air behind her right ear, "but I just can't seem to grasp it and pull it in. So frustrating."

"Yes," I said.

"Now, over there is someone who has been waiting patiently to speak with you. I'll go and see about lunch."

We had come to the edge of her garden, a beautiful square of ground at the top of the hill. At its border, the stone path changed to white gravel and wandered through groupings of blooming flowers and dark greenery, everything arranged carefully to suggest no arrangement at all. At the center of the garden was a tall stone birdbath, nearly as green with age as the ivy at its base. A person who had been waiting patiently for me was tossing pebbles into the water of the bath.

Amanda looked up as my steps sounded on the gravel. I was happy to see her smile, although that smile also cost me something, as it was Mary's smile in miniature. "Mary, Jr.," Harry used to call Amanda, and it was true. She was sturdier than her mother had been, and her blonde hair had yet to darken to Mary's honey color, but the resemblance was striking. It was the eyes, I decided, and something behind the eyes.

"Hello, Uncle Owen," she said, using an honorary title bestowed by Mary and resented by Harry.

"Hello," I said. This was the first time I had seen Amanda since the day of her mother's funeral, and then it had been at a distance. It occurred to me that I should say some correct, consoling word to her now, but none came to me.

Amanda consoled me, instead. "My mommy's in heaven," she said.

Together we walked to a concrete bench at the far end of the garden. Amanda brushed it off carefully. I noted that her orange shorts had already borne the brunt of her gardening and decided that she was worried about my bargain suit. I lifted her onto the bench and sat down beside her. A steady breeze from the ocean made the full sun of the garden tolerable. We watched a large bee moving from flower to flower, its yellow pollen sacs clearly visible on its black legs. I was thinking of Harry and so, as it happened, was Amanda.

"My daddy's away," she said. "Do you know where he is?"

"Sort of," I said, not wanting to admit to Amanda that I'd lost track of Harry.

"I need you to tell him something," Amanda said. "I want to go home."

I looked down at her, afraid I would see the beginnings of tears, but her expression was simply very serious, as though she was trying to impress me with the importance of the request. The objections I had been prepared to make to her grandfather came to mind again. I was too involved emotionally, too numb myself from Mary's death, too resentful of Harry, the survivor. None of the excuses seemed worth speaking aloud.

I was picky about my clients. Harry hadn't asked me and Harold Ohlman, Sr., didn't appeal to me. But Amanda Ohlman was another matter. Mary, Jr., sat watching me now, not arguing or persuading, just outlasting me, as her mother always had.

"You win, kiddo," I said. "I'll take the case."

THREE

"DID YOU SAY my dad sent you?" Harry asked me.

It was the afternoon of the day Harry fell. I'd put away my disguises and stopped by to see him. This was another brilliant idea of mine. I'd decided that I could safely visit Harry once a week or so, telling him that I'd driven down from Red Bank. I had made the first of these visits on the day I arrived in Spring Lake. I'd been anxious to talk with Harry, to check firsthand what Mr. Ohlman had called his son's "spiritual crisis." I'd also wanted to give Harry a chance to talk to me, hoping that he might clear up the mystery of his isolation if an old friend just asked him about it. I'd been disappointed in that hope. On my first visit, Harry hadn't greeted me like an old friend. He'd been sullen and withdrawn. We'd had a beer while we stared at each other. Then I left. Now, on my second call, I found Harry suddenly inquisitive.

"Your dad let me know you were down here," I said. "He asked me to look in on you." My experience with lying had taught me that it was best to play only minor variations on the truth.

Harry grunted. "It's hard to imagine Dad calling you, Owen. He never thought that much of you."

Or my suits, I almost added.

"You sure it wasn't my mother?" Harry asked.

"I have spoken with her," I said cautiously.

"That sounds more like it." Harry was grimly proud of his small, incorrect deduction. "She used to send me holy cards in boarding school when I was sick." The memory didn't gladden him, and, as the current representative of the holy cards, I was duly offended.

"I hope I don't need a note from your mother to visit you, Harry," I said. "I am your friend." I must have been looking for an excuse to drop the whole thing, handing Harry a straight line like that.

He passed on it. "Sorry," he said. "I'm bad company. How's your beer holding up?"

It was still half full, but I got up from my chair and went off to retrieve another round. Harry held his empty can out for me to take as I passed. I left the living room and made my way through the small dining room and into the even smaller kitchen, which was at the very back of the house. When I was safely inside the kitchen, I held Harry's empty can upside down over the sink. There on the bottom in pencil were my own initials. Early the previous Friday, while Harry had been taking his walk, I'd searched his cottage. I had found very little of Harry's own in the rented house and nothing out of the ordinary. Before I'd left, I'd played a hunch and marked Harry's beer cans like a scientist tagging birds to study population levels.

I took two cold, initialed beers from the nearly empty refrigerator and returned to the living room. Harry's cottage was tiny but well-appointed, with little of the cheap nautical decor common in shore rentals. The living room had a formal fireplace, which Harry had decorated with a quart of Chivas Regal. I discreetly checked the mark I'd made on the bottle's label as I passed. It told me that the level of scotch hadn't changed. In addition to the fireplace, the room contained a sofa and chair, both upholstered in a tired green, and a coffee table, which held a large, empty ashtray of dark blue glass. On the wall behind Harry's head hung a series of small woodblock prints, among them a Gothic church, an English village, and a stylized forest. The prints each had a black ink sky that made them look like photo negatives.

Harry was sitting sideways on the sofa with his bad leg propped up. He was wearing shorts, and I couldn't help studying the red scar left by his operation. It ran from near his ankle almost to his knee. The leg itself looked swollen and pink.

"Your leg bothering you today?" I asked as I handed Harry his beer.

"Just sore," Harry said. "I tried to do too much this morning."

"How are you otherwise?" I asked.

Harry addressed the top of his beer can. "Fine," he said. "Couldn't be better." He spoke without rancor or irony or conviction. A stupid answer for a stupid question.

During the silence that followed, I considered the man sitting on the sofa before me. When Harry and I had first met as college freshmen, nineteen long years earlier, I'd thought of him as incredibly lucky. Well off financially, smarter than his lazy grades suggested, facile at sports, gifted in music and art, Harry had been someone to look up to and envy. There were stray dark spots in the picture—his father's insistence on dictating his son's future was one—but when Harry won Mary, it seemed to me one notable triumph in a lifetime destined for triumph. After law school, Harry joined his father's firm, where I had worked for him briefly. About the time I resigned, Harry had taken the business over completely. From the occasional news

I'd received from Mary over the years, I knew that the firm had prospered under Harry. I'd assumed that he had been prospering, too.

He wore those years of prosperity badly now, like a slept-in tuxedo. His dark, thinning hair was disheveled, and the paunch that he'd once worked so hard to master was now a simple statement of fact. There was nothing apparent of his old charm or the easy smile that used to highlight his regular features. The broad, fixed smile that had so irritated me on our morning walk was also missing. His expression as I watched him was alternately listless and wary, as he forgot me and then noticed that I was still with him.

I decided that I had had enough of the room's dusty silence. "I was trying to remember a poem on the drive down here," I said. "I read it years ago. About a bird and the ocean. Ring a bell?" This was my artless attempt to identify the shadowy poem that somehow reminded Harry's mother of his situation. Perhaps the poem had been a childhood favorite of Harry's. Perhaps he was acting out some memory of it here at the Jersey shore.

"Don't ask me," Harry said. "You were the English major."

"The late sixties was a bad time to pick up a grounding in the classics," I said. "Our favorite poem was 'Hell no, we won't go.'"

Harry drifted off for a moment on some memory of those lost days. He escaped the reverie by shaking his head like a man coming out of the water. "Before you go, I want to show you something," he said. He got up from the sofa with an effort and limped off down the hallway that led to the cottage's two bedrooms and the tiny bath. "Come on," he called over his shoulder.

He led me to the first bedroom, which he'd converted to a studio. Charcoal sketches on newsprint covered the walls. An empty easel stood next to the single window. A wooden case of paints rested beside it.

"What do you think?" Harry asked.

I circled the room, pausing at each sketch. They were done in the heavy, slashing style that I remembered well from our college days. Harry sketched in bold, repetitive strokes, no one of which stood out as the true, indispensable line. In the more successful sketches, the angry competition of the strokes disappeared and the subject emerged. The subjects in Harry's current gallery were all recognizable Spring Lake landmarks. The lake itself, with and without footbridge, appeared more than once on the newsprint sheets, along with several of the eccentric local houses and other buildings. Harry's dark sketch of St. Brigid's reminded me of the way the church had appeared that morning in the mist.

There was one notable local subject missing from the gallery. "Where's the ocean?" I asked.

"I'm working up to it," Harry said. "So what do you think of my studio?"

I thought that there was little to show for the time he'd spent in the town. That criticism reminded me of Mr. Ohlman's assessment of Harry's painting: it was something he used as an excuse to put off other things. "It doesn't smell right," I finally said. "Where's the turpentine smell and the linseed oil? Your dad said you came down here to paint."

"I did," Harry said. "I haven't found a subject yet."

"Any of these would do," I said, indicating the sketches with a wave of my beer can. "A painting's not a subject. It's how you paint the subject."

"May I quote you?" Harry was working his way up from irritated to mad.

"I'm quoting you, I think," I said. "I was the sounding board back at Boston, remember. I was the one you kept up nights talking about how you were going to be the next Gauguin." I was trying to get mad myself, for no reason I could identify. I'd once told Harry that our friendship consisted of a series of affronts, that we took turns being mad at one another. Now both of us were mad at the same time, and there was no future in that. I adopted a less hostile tone. "Your sketches are good," I said. "Now you should get your brushes wet."

Harry turned toward the door. "There's no hurry," he said.

He led me back out into the living room. He didn't sit down when he got there, and I was content to take the hint.

"I guess I'll head back," I said.

"What's the drive like from Red Bank?" Harry asked. The question might have worried me, had Harry's tone not told me that he was just trying, belatedly, to make conversation.

"About half an hour on the Parkway," I said as we stepped out onto the front porch.

"When's the last time you stayed at the shore?" Harry's questioning was still disinterested. Now that he'd gotten me to leave, he seemed to want a few more minutes of my company.

I had to think about his question. "It was back in high school," I said. "A summer retreat at Seaside Park."

"The famous retreat where you found religion?" Harry knew my history as well as I knew his.

"That's the one," I said.

"I think I found religion every time I saw the ocean when I was growing up," Harry said. "Especially during high school, when I was starting to doubt. Something about the ocean would make me think there might be a God after all. If it was around sunset and the sky had a soft violet to it and the water was a blue green, I'd be sure God existed. I'd get all fired up about how good I was going to be and how I was going to change my life. Then I'd go home and start screwing up all over again."

We were moving slowly down the front walk, paced by Harry's bad leg. Before I could decide what to make of his sudden confidence, the moment passed. "Why the hell don't you buy a decent car?" he asked me.

This was in reference to my '65 Karmann-Ghia, which sat rusting at the curb before us. I'd rented a featureless Chevrolet for my surveillance work, but I'd been careful to swap it for my own car before visiting Harry. "I'm waiting to pay this one off," I said.

I then remembered some other business I wanted to do that day. "As long as I'm down here, I think I'll nose around a bit," I said. "That old church looks interesting."

I had turned to gesture toward the church when I first saw her. It was the kind of first sight that comes back to haunt you. A tall, slender young woman, she was walking along the lake bank in a graceful amble

that had nothing to do with exercise. She seemed unconcerned with the scenery and equally indifferent
about being scenery herself, which was remarkable,
considering that her outfit consisted predominantly of
a barely adequate tee shirt and extremely adequate
legs. Her short brown hair was cut and combed like a
boy's, complete with cowlick, but that was the only
boyish thing about her and the only awkward thing. I
watched until she entered the small grove of trees at
the northern end of the lake.

"Who is that?" I asked.

"Don't know," Harry said in a tone that suggested
he had reconciled himself to my departure.

"Whoever she is, she has single-handedly revised
my opinion of this town as a tourist attraction."

"You'd better stick to the church tour," Harry said.
"It's more your speed."

That slight was encouragingly like the old Harry. I
looked up as I climbed into my car, hoping to catch
him smiling at my expense. Instead I found that he was
already gazing toward the front door of his cottage.

"See you later," I said.

"So long," Harry replied.

FOUR

AFTER LEAVING Harry, I drove to St. Brigid's. I wasn't looking for a tour of the church. I was going to meet Father Peter Marruca, the sole priest serving the aging parish, which had grown far too small for its grand church. Mr. Ohlman had told me that he'd been in contact with the priest, that Father Peter had been trying to counsel Harry, and that I should look him up. I was finally getting around to that now.

I parked on a side street behind St. Brigid's, out of sight of Harry's cottage. The rectory was modest in comparison with the church that shaded it. The house was also old, its red brick pitted and cracked. I looked around the front porch for an electric doorbell and settled for a manual one mounted in the center of the door itself. It consisted of a butterfly-shaped key set on a discolored brass dome. Turning the key vigorously produced a grinding noise and a tiny, vestigial ring.

The ringing did not produce Father Marruca. I tried the front door and found that it was open. As I stuck my head inside the dark hallway, I was struck by associations that crowded back as far as my altar-boy days. I felt an impulse to shut the door quietly and go back to my car. I shook it off and called out, "Hello! Anybody home?"

The answering call came from far down the hallway. "Back here to your right."

I had begun forming a mental picture of Father Marruca, based on the evidence of his ancient rectory. I saw him as gray and bent from years of service, but wise also, a man for whom this world held no more surprises. In other words, I was compiling a wish list, conjuring up the person I thought I needed to take Harry's problem off my unwilling shoulders.

When I arrived at the open office door, I found a man my own age, if not younger, seated behind a cluttered desk. He was wearing a bright red golf shirt, and there were sunglasses pushed up onto his dark hair. It took the physical evidence of the nameplate on the desk top to convince me that I'd found Peter Marruca. He was speaking on the phone, or rather listening to someone else speak. He waved me into the room without looking up. I studied the priest from the vantage point of an armchair much older than either of us. He was thin, with the angular jaw and high cheekbones of a storybook Indian. He had blue eyes overshadowed by a slightly protruding brow. His high, narrow forehead was unmarked by age, but it carried a small, red scar than ran upwards from his left eyebrow at an angle. As he listened to the unseen caller, he massaged the scar with his fingertips in a circular motion.

Finally, the priest interrupted the speaker. "Your faith shouldn't depend on the Virgin Mary turning somebody's rosary beads to gold, or some other silly miracle." He looked up at me and shook his head. "I'm sorry you feel that way. Look," he said, "someone's come in. Can you call back? Okay." He set the phone down firmly. "Sorry," he said to me. "I'm short-fused sometimes. That was one of my more colorful parishioners. Sweet little old lady, but she thinks the world has gone to hell in a hand basket since they dropped the Latin mass.

"So, what can I do for you?"

"My name is Owen Keane," I began. It turned out to be all I needed to say.

"Owen Keane," Father Peter repeated. "I've been expecting you. Harold Ohlman called two weeks ago to say you'd be stopping by. Did you just get into town?"

"No," I said. "I've been here a week. Settling in."

"You must have gotten pretty settled to have gone unnoticed for a week in this burg. So you're Mr. Ohlman's watchdog." The priest leaned back in his chair and then sat up again quickly. He pulled a wrinkled golf glove from his back pants pocket and tossed it onto the desk. "I've been anxious to meet you. He told me a lot about you over the phone. I've been wondering how much of it is true."

"You can generally count on Mr. Ohlman's accuracy." If not his tact, I added to myself.

"Really?" The priest smiled in friendly amazement. "I mean, some of it's a little farfetched. You studied for the priesthood, I understand."

"Yes," I said.

"But you gave it up."

"Yes."

"Did you have doubts?"

"I had questions." There was a time when this line of inquiry would have reduced me to an embarrassed silence, but I'd grown more thick-skinned over the years. Even so, as Father Peter's blue eyes smiled at me, my old leather armchair began to feel as cozy as any laboratory slide.

"Now you're what?" the priest asked. "An investigator? Mr. Ohlman made it sound a little mystical, like you're looking for God in cheap motels and down dark alleys."

"I'm still looking for answers to my questions," I said. "Dark alleys are as good a place to look as any."

He nodded like a co-conspirator. "I agree, Owen. One place is as good as another for that kind of question. Even sleepy Spring Lake. Do you expect to find a clue or two down here?"

"That or work on my golf game."

The priest laughed. "Touché. Aside from my temper, golf is my one bad habit. Priests need one or two, Owen, just like everybody else. You don't mind first names, I hope. I prefer 'Peter' to 'Father,' myself."

"Fine," I said.

"I should tell you something about my own background," Peter said. "So we start out even. I had questions myself when I was in the seminary, but they must not have been as fundamental as yours. They mostly involved authority. Respect for authority. I still have problems in that area, which is bad news for someone who has taken holy orders." His voice was light and slightly nasal, but not unpleasant. He looked up at the ceiling as he spoke, which gave his confidences an impersonal, public quality. "My outlet for my questioning is writing. Poetry, plays, some political stuff. I think I have that last category to thank for my current posting. I did a series of articles on Central America that really frosted the Archbishop. He's an old Republican at heart, maybe even a Whig. When he called to tell me that Father Palladay, the previous pastor here, had taken ill and that I was going to replace him, he made it sound like an opportunity to do penance."

He raised a disorganized pile of papers from his desk. "I'm working on something less controversial now. It's a history of St. Brigid's. I thought writing it might make me feel more at home in Spring Lake." He paused for a beat to consider that idea with a wistful smile. "Our church is a memorial to a young girl named Brigid Kelly who drowned in the lake just after the turn of the century. Her father, who must have been as rich as two Kennedys, commissioned the church in her memory. The old guy overdid it in my estimation. It's a scaled-down version of St. Peter's Basilica, as you may have noticed."

"How did the girl come to drown?" I asked.

Peter pulled the pile of paper toward him. "You'll find out when you buy the book," he said and laughed. "That's probably enough local gossip anyway, at least of the ancient variety. I'm sure you'd rather be discussing Harry Ohlman. I've got about ten minutes till my next appointment. Ask me anything you want."

He made the offer of ten minutes sound generous, but it left me at a loss for where to begin. "I understand you've spoken with Harry," I finally said.

"A couple of times. I'd noticed him before his father called to ask for my help. Harry's been a regular at our early Sunday service this summer. It's a thin crowd usually, and Harry stands out in it like a bear in a flock of sheep. It isn't just that he's thirty years younger than most of the others. He really gets into the mass. He's always either kneeling with his head in his hands or staring up at the altar like Jesus is waving at him from the crucifix.

"Anyway, Harry's father called one day to ask me to look in on his son. Incidentally, Mr. Ohlman spoke as though he knows my Archbishop personally."

And the skeletons in his closet, I thought. Out loud I said, "I wouldn't be surprised."

Peter was impressed. "I stopped Harry one Sunday after mass and asked if he'd mind a visit. We've talked several times since then. I haven't found out much that his father didn't already know—namely, that his son has been absolutely devastated by his wife's death. Obviously that wasn't enough to satisfy Mr. Ohlman, since he's added you to the roster."

He checked his watch quickly. "Frankly, Owen, I think he's wasting his money and your time. He wants Harry over his grief, but there isn't anything you or I can do to speed that process. I told Mr. Ohlman to give him more time."

"What did he say to that?"

"He wanted to know how much time we were talking about, as though it were a negotiable item." Peter shook his head. "I told him that people heal at different rates." He picked up a stack of mail from his desk and began to sort it into two piles. "That goes for spiritual healing as well as physical healing. I'm distrustful of any grieving theory that sets the same deadline for everyone." He tossed the larger pile into the wastebasket next to his desk. "It strikes me as too pat, too glib."

"I know the feeling," I said.

"That's a danger when you start to treat human behavior like a predictable science. Although that may just be jealousy speaking. It bugs me that social scientists have assumed my rightful prerogatives."

"As a priest?"

"No. I meant my prerogatives as a writer. That's where people traditionally turned when they wanted some insight into human behavior. To literature. Now they look in a textbook. No wonder we're all screwed up. The artists have surrendered the high ground to the Ph.D.s."

The priest's long aside reminded me of the poem that haunted Harry's mother and now nagged at me. I asked him about it.

"A poem about a bird and the ocean? Sorry, it doesn't ring a bell. I have a hard enough time keeping track of the stuff I write myself."

Peter looked at his watch again and decided to get back to the point. "You say you've been here a week? What have you been up to?"

I described the process of watching Harry's movements, which had been few, and noting his local contacts, which so far had been none. I also told Peter about my visits to Harry, my phony day trips from Red Bank, and about how I'd burgled Harry's cottage one morning while he had been taking his walk.

Peter smiled at his lap during my recitation and massaged the scar on his forehead. "How did you manage to break in, or is that a professional secret?"

"I didn't have to," I said. "Harry left his front door open."

"Have you made any discoveries?"

"Just negative ones. Harry doesn't seem to be doing any painting, which is his excuse for being down here. Mr. Ohlman thought Harry might be drinking heavily. I'm pretty sure that's not true."

"What makes you think so?" Peter asked.

"I inventoried Harry's booze supply when I searched his place last week. It was pretty much intact today. He drinks openly when I visit him. He just doesn't seem to be drinking when he's alone.''

I paused at this point, wondering whether I should mention Mr. Ohlman's other concern to the priest. In the end, my desire to discuss the situation with someone was too great. "Harry's dad is also worried about drugs," I said.

Peter nodded soberly. "That's a real possibility these days, I'm afraid. I haven't seen any signs of that though. Have you?''

"Not exactly. I didn't find anything when I searched his cottage. But Harry is acting strangely. He's distant with me. Wary. It may just be that I remind him of the old days. It may be that anything or anybody he associates with Mary is too much for him.

"It's almost too much for me," I added. A week of keeping my own counsel had made me free with my secrets. "It's more than just old memories in my case. I'm feeling more and more hostile toward Harry. I seem to be blaming him for Mary's death, which is crazy.''

"Why is it crazy?" I'd finally succeeded in getting the priest's full attention. He leaned forward in his chair with his hands folded together on the desk.

"The accident wasn't Harry's fault. The other driver ran a red light. He's in jail now waiting for his trial.''

"You've investigated the accident?''

"No. I read about it at the time it happened. And I've spoken with Mary's parents.''

"If you don't mind a suggestion, I think you should look into the accident more deeply. Call it a hunch, but sitting in a confessional for hours on end gives a person an ear for guilt. I get a feeling sometimes when

I talk with Harry that there's guilt mixed up with his grief. It may just be an irrational reaction on his part. I mean, he may be blaming himself because he happened to be driving the car that night. But there could be more to it.''

"I'll look into it," I said, grateful to have a practical line to follow.

"Good." Peter emphasized the judgment by slapping the desk top with both palms. The gesture also signaled the end of our interview. "If I think of anything else, I'll get in touch. Where are you staying?"

"The Gascony Inn," I said as I stood up.

The priest stood, too, and I was surprised to find myself looking down at him. "I'll see you out," he said. "Then maybe I can get changed. My three o'clock is a young lady thinking of converting to the faith. It might be better if I looked the part."

He paused in the doorway to his office. It occurred to me that this lone priest might be happy to have a confidant himself for a change. "This convert's name is Diana Lord. She's our local mystery woman. No one in town seems to know much about her, except that she has money. She's rented an expensive house on Ocean Avenue. I've only spoken with her twice, but I've gotten a sense that something's not quite right with her, that she's troubled in some way."

"What do you mean?" I asked.

"She told me that she changed her mind about getting married recently. I think she might have changed it while she was walking down the aisle. She's certainly running away from something in her recent past. It's just another hunch of mine, but I think her problem could make your pal Harry's situation seem straightforward."

From down the hallway came the faint, grinding ring of the old bell. Peter grimaced. "So much for changing."

He led the way down the creaking hallway. When he opened the front door for me, I found myself face to face with the young woman I'd seen walking the lake shore. Her large eyes were gray, I could see now, and steady. I guessed her age to be about twenty-five. She had exchanged her tee shirt and bathing suit for a blouse and shorts, but her cowlicked hair was unchanged. So was her cool indifference to my examination. It was an attitude I couldn't hope to match.

"Hello," I said as I moved to one side of the entry way.

Her only reply was a momentary movement of her wide mouth that fell short of being a smile. She stepped past me with a silent, graceful motion that seemed less material than the trace of perfume that lingered behind her.

I found Father Peter grinning up at me from his post by the door. "Good day, Mr. Keane," he said.

FIVE

HARRY DID NOT appear for his walk the next morning. I stretched for fifteen minutes under my maple tree by the lake before I decided that he was probably giving his bad leg a rest. I elected to jog without him. I was dressed for it, after all. For variety, I headed north toward Spring Lake's tiny business district. I padded past a block of small, touristy shops that ended at an intersection shared by a practical-looking corner drug store and the town's combination municipal building and fire station. There was also a fifties-style liquor store that the neo-Victorians at work all over Spring Lake must have dearly loved. It had a flat, round roof edged in stainless steel and topped by a neon sign shaped like the fin of a tall, thin shark. I was on a first-name basis with Tom, the manager of the liquor store, having passed him a little of Mr. Ohlman's money to tell me about Harry's booze purchases. I turned right at the intersection and headed for the beach. When I reached the boardwalk, I dropped my pace to a stroll and fell into examining the walkers and runners who were sharing the morning with me.

While I strolled, I watched for Harry to appear, on the off chance that he'd beaten me out of the blocks this morning. I was also watching for Diana Lord, the sad-eyed woman I'd almost met at Father Peter's the day before. Her problem was more mysterious than Harry's, according to the priest. I decided that Fa-

ther Peter really meant he found the woman more interesting than Harry, a fact I resented for Harry's
sake, but understood completely. Diana Lord was already much in my own thoughts that morning, quietly shoving poor Harry aside, Peter's implied
warning, that she offered difficulties darker and
deeper than Harry's, never came to mind.

The day had taken on a laid-back, vacation quality. I'd called Mr. Ohlman the afternoon before to report my lack of progress and to push Father Peter's
judgment that all Harry needed was more time, Mr.
Ohlman hadn't bought it. He'd been more enthusiastic when I'd asked for information concerning the accident. Perhaps like me he was hungry for a chance to
do something practical. He had promised me copies of
the accident reports and had offered to set up an interview with the couple who had entertained Mary and
Harry that night. I had a sense that I could play
hookey until that information arrived, a feeling that
made Harry's nonappearance this morning seem like
part of the program.

I walked for half an hour without seeing Harry or
the mystery woman. Then I returned to the Gascony
Inn. I paused for a moment on the short front walk to
check the progress of the house painting that had been
defiling the salt air since I'd arrived in town. The dark
olive exterior was finished, and it almost shone in the
morning light. The painters, who had not yet arrived
for the day, had turned their attention to the broad
front porch. Its ceiling had been painted gray. The last
step, I deduced from reading the labels of paint cans
stacked on the porch, would be to paint its wide-plank
flooring a dark red. I entered the inn through the
heavy front door as quietly as I could and climbed to

my third-floor room. That room had first attracted me to the Gascony, as it commanded a view of half the lake and of Harry's cottage.

The room was expensive by my standards. It was furnished in a heavy, uncomfortable suite of walnut with burl inlays. The headboard of the bed had a high, formal pediment like the front of a Roman temple. The room was papered and carpeted in authentic Victorian patterns that were dark and incredibly busy. In addition to the view it offered, I'd been attracted to the room by its steep rent. I had decided to spend Mr. Ohlman's money freely, until he thought twice about my unique qualifications for this assignment. Toward the end, I'd bought a handsome piece of surveillance equipment, a Nikon camera equipped with a telephoto lens only slightly smaller and lighter than a beer keg. I set the camera up on its tripod as soon as I got up to the room. Then I spent a few minutes studying the peeling paint on Harry's front door. All was quiet on that front.

I showered in my tiny bathroom, which appeared to have been overlooked in the general renovation of the house. I suspected that the room had originally been a large closet, promoted to its current job sometime around the First World War. I based my estimate on the exposed pipes, the claw-foot bathtub, and the water pressure, or lack thereof.

On my way down to breakfast, I met George Metelis, my landlord. He and his wife had bought the inn in the hope of retiring from the 9-to-5 rut, but so far only Metelis had made good his escape. Mrs. Metelis, whom I seldom saw, still commuted daily to a programming job in Freehold. George Metelis was a friendly man with close-cropped hair and large red ears that he scratched and pulled nervously whenever we talked. His ears got a break this morning, as their owner's arms were full of clean towels.

"Morning," Metelis said. He examined me carefully, as he always did. My activities in Spring Lake were a source of much interest for my landlord. So far, I had managed to keep him in the dark. "Enjoy your breakfast," he said as he passed me on the stairs. "There's a little added attraction this morning."

"Warm toast?" I asked.

He chuckled good-naturedly. "Better than that."

Because the Gascony had been a guesthouse in an earlier manifestation, it had a large dining room. It was also a pleasant room, lit by a wall of windows. Metelis and his wife had furnished it in white wicker, and it was open to the public as well as to guests of the inn. I stopped short of the dining room's threshold. From there I could see the added attraction my landlord had promised me. It was Diana Lord, alone at a table, backlit by the eastern windows.

She was sitting profile toward me, holding an unlit cigarette. The long sleeves of her blue cotton shirt were rolled back a turn or two to expose her slim brown arms. The few other early patrons of the dining room seemed to be aware of her, even those who were pointedly ignoring her. Or was I imagining that she had somehow organized the room around her? Certainly Shelly, the Gascony's lone waitress, who had noticed her. Shelly looked across to me from the kitchen doorway and grinned. Her grin reminded me of Father Peter's reaction from the day before, when I'd bungled my first meeting with Diana. I was determined to do better this morning. Here was a genuine opportunity to evade my responsibilities, and I didn't hesitate.

As I strode across the dining room to her table, I was conscious of a feeling of suspense, due in part to the excitement of waiting to hear the stupid remark that would shortly pop from my mouth. Diana made the job of meeting her easier by turning her head as I stepped up to her table and smiling. It was a real smile this time, although her eyes retained their steady sadness. In combination, her eyes and smile conveyed the flattering idea that my sudden appearance was a momentary distraction from some constant worry.

"Good morning," I said with no more than a trace of my usual awkwardness. "I didn't get a chance to introduce myself yesterday. My name is Owen Keane."

"I know," she said. "Peter told me." She either knew or assumed that the priest had also told me her name, because she didn't offer it. Her speech was as casual as her outfit. Her voice was higher and softer than I'd expected. I revised my estimate of her age downward to nineteen or twenty. "I'm just having coffee," she said.

The remark puzzled me for a moment, as there was no coffee on her table. I finally realized that she was asking me to join her. Shelly arrived at my elbow, her timing perfect. "Two coffees, please," I said. I ignored Shelly's broad nod, the equivalent of a poke in the ribs. She and I had become friends over the course of a lonely week, but I didn't want a rooting section right now.

I sat down opposite Diana, admiring her tan and the golden highlights in her hair while I tried to think of my next line. The two activities, admiring and thinking, turned out to be incompatible, and I'd made no progress by the time Shelly arrived with the coffee.

It didn't matter. After Shelly had delivered two fragile-looking antique cups and saucers, Diana leaned toward me slightly. "Peter told me you were an investigator," she said.

"I guess that's right," I said. Years of explaining to strangers my occupation, or rather my preoccupation, hadn't made me any better at it, a sign that I didn't understand it completely myself. My conversation with the priest was fresh in my mind. "I look for answers to questions," I said.

Diana thought about that for a long, serious moment. It gave me time to note that her gray eyes were flecked with brown. Then she said, "Would they care if we went out on the porch?" She waved her unlit cigarette by way of an explanation.

I picked up both coffees and followed her through open French doors that led onto the side porch. Diana had her cigarette burning before she'd gotten two steps from the door. She sat on the wooden railing of the porch with her long legs crossed. I sat in the only chair that happened to face her, still holding a cup and saucer in each hand.

I was certain by then that Diana Lord's arrival at the Gascony had not been a happy accident. Peter had given her enough information on me to interest her. Now she was trying to make up her mind to ask for my help.

At that moment, the painters came around the corner of the house. They were two college kids who were working and partying their way through a summer at the shore. At the sight of Diana, they stopped in their tracks and grinned appreciatively. She was less pleased to see them. She tossed her cigarette into a flower bed below her and stood up.

I stood, too, helplessly balancing the antique cups.

"I'll be back," Diana said. She walked slowly between the two painters, who suddenly looked like large, paint-splattered boys, and disappeared around the corner of the porch.

SIX

THAT AFTERNOON I spotted Harry on his way to the beach. I should be honest and admit that Shelly, my waitress friend from the Gascony, actually spotted him as she was getting off work. I had shared the bare outline of my mission with Shelly because I felt I could trust her and because I needed another pair of eyes. She was eager to help. She thought I was a real detective, someone who knew what he was doing. I needed that, too.

Shelly found me in my room, where I was passing my self-bestowed day off by reading a Dorothy Sayers paperback. After I'd thanked Shelly for the information and told her that I would follow it up, she lingered in my doorway. Shelly was in her late twenties, but she seemed older than that. She was divorced and lived with her parents in Belmar, the shore town north of Spring Lake. With her parents' help, she was raising two boys, whose pictures she had proudly shown me during our first talk. The way she was looking at me now made me think that she had mentally adopted a third.

"Did you enjoy your coffee this morning?" Shelly finally asked me.

I knew then that she was curious about Diana Lord. There was a lot of that going around.

"A prospective client," I said, expressing my fond but slight hope.

"Is that all?"

"Outside of my dreams."

Shelly would not be coaxed into repeating her grin of this morning. "Watch yourself," she said. "I've been thinking it over. You could be asking for trouble with that one."

"Trouble and I go back years," I said in my private-eye voice. It didn't go over very well. I might have been out of tune from listening to Peter Wimsey's prattle instead of Philip Marlowe's drawl. Or it might just have been that, of the two of us, Shelly was the better detective.

"Watch yourself," she repeated.

I promised, carelessly, that I would. After she'd gone, I changed into a variation of my jogger disguise, substituting bathing trunks for my running shorts and a wide-brimmed straw hat for my neon cap. I zinc-oxided my long nose, grabbed a towel and Lord Peter, and headed out in search of Harry.

He wasn't hard to spot. I found him sitting on the edge of the elevated boardwalk just north of the bathing pavilion. His legs dangled over the beach, and an oversized sketch pad rested on his knees. Harry's subject was an old rock breakwater that ran twenty yards or so out into the sea. The rocks were black where they weren't covered with dark green seaweed. Two young boys balanced on the rocks at a point just short of the surf line, waiting for the lifeguard to whistle them in. Harry was slashing away at his pad with a bit of charcoal. There was an apple on the boards next to him, which suggested an extended effort.

Seeing Harry's apple reminded me that I hadn't eaten lunch. I climbed to the top of the old bathing pavilion, a sturdy cement cube built right on the sand.

The pavilion held changing rooms and showers. An open-sided shelter house sat on the building's flat roof. I bought an ice cream cone at the shelter's concession stand and sat down on a gritty bench. Over the top of my paperback, I watched Harry work.

Passers-by on the boardwalk slowed as they came up to Harry and discreetly examined his sketch. This brought back a memory from our freshman year at Boston College. In those days, Harry had used sketching as a way of meeting women. He had routinely begun to draw whenever he was waiting for a class to start or while we lounged on some grassy quad between classes. The technique had often worked. There was something about the quiet activity that invited curiosity. As a bonus, the sketch itself had always provided an impersonal topic for an ice-breaking conversation.

The old dodge was working now. Two women had paused behind Harry, easing the straps of their large canvas beach bags from their shoulders as they compared his effort with the original. If Harry had turned in feigned surprise, smiled shyly, and said hello, it would have made my old Boston memory complete. Instead, he tore the sketch from his pad and crumpled it into a ball. His audience shouldered their burdens and left him.

The flies that had been coveting my ice cream were now biting at my bare ankles. I left the shelter and descended to the beach itself, passing through a gate where a teenager lounging under a large umbrella checked my plastic beach badge. I spread my towel on the hot sand and lay on my stomach, holding my open book an inch or two below the brim of my hat. By moving to the beach, I had entered the edge of Harry's peripheral vision, but I had improved my own view as well. I could see Harry's face in profile now, as he alternately squinted at the rocks and water and stared down at his pad. Harry was not enjoying himself. He had the look of a man who was struggling against unexpected odds. His face glistened with sweat, which he wiped off occasionally with the back of his drawing arm. The sweat also ran down his dangling legs, making his scar look like a fresh wound. As I watched, Harry pulled the second sketch from the pad, balled it up, and sent it to join the first. He took no time to regroup, but began his slashing attack immediately on a fresh sheet.

I rolled over onto my back and examined the scenery. The blue shadow of a large ship could just be seen on the horizon. A mile or two off shore, a sailboat was making its way slowly north, its mainsail painfully white in the bright sunlight. The ocean had taken on the inviting light green-blue color of a swimming pool. In the foreground there were bobbing heads of a dozen swimmers and, closer still, a crowd of waders and shell hunters—mostly children—stood in the gentle surf.

When I looked back to Harry, he was getting to his feet unsteadily, like a beaten boxer. His third attempt at the sketch was now a wad of paper that he clutched in one fist. He retrieved his first two efforts, using his pad like a dustpan, and carried them to a nearby trash can. He stuffed the sketches in and, as an afterthought, he tore the pad in two and pushed it in after them.

By the time I had climbed to the boardwalk, Harry was across Ocean Avenue, limping off in the direction of his cottage. I retrieved his half-eaten apple, which he had left lying where he'd sat. I used the apple as a prop, as my excuse to cross stage right to the trash container. There I deposited the apple and withdrew, in exchange, the three crumpled sketches. I crumpled these further by rolling them up in my sandy beach towel. Then I set off for the Gascony.

The front steps of the inn had been roped off by the painters, who had managed to finish half the porch floor before heading for the ocean. I used a side stairway near the spot where Diana Lord and I had had our brief encounter that morning. There I met Metelis, my landlord. He was happy to see me.

"Too early to splice the main brace?" he asked. This was his nautical way of asking if I wanted a drink. One of the daily services provided by the Gascony Inn was a complimentary glass of wine.

"Fine by my watch," I said.

Metelis nodded and disappeared into the house. I used the waiting time to shake out my towel and to smooth out what was left of Harry's sketches. It was easy to place the three in order. He must have worked on the first one for some time before I'd found him; it was nearly a finished product. Aside from some small perspective problems, I thought the drawing was as good or better than any I'd seen in his cottage the day before. Harry had managed to suggest both the jagged solidity of the black rocks and its opposite, the translucent movement of the water. The second sketch was a poor imitation of the first, with no more than the bare outlines worked out by the combative strokes. The third sketch was in pieces, both literally and figuratively, Harry having torn it up. The pieces I had held only unrelated, angry lines, as though the second sketch had been disassembled and scattered about the page.

I was still trying to see the sense behind the sequence of drawings when Metelis reappeared carrying two large wine-glasses filled to their brims. He also carried a package, tucked under one arm.

"This came for you today," he said. He set the glasses down gingerly before handing me the padded mailer. It bore the gaudy colors and logo of an overnight delivery service. The label told me that it had come from Ohlman, Pulsifer, and Hurst. My copies of the accident reports no doubt, dispatched by the ever-efficient Ms. Kiefner.

Metelis looked disappointed when I set the package down unopened next to my chair. He consoled himself by sniffing aggressively at his pale yellow wine. "I think you'll like this one," he said.

This remark was part of a daily charade Metelis performed for his guests. It was based on the idea that his free wine came from dusty bottles stored deep in the Gascony's basement. I'd learned from Shelly that the wine actually flowed from large cardboard containers with plastic spigots that resided in a kitchen refrigerator.

I went along with the gag by testing the wine's bouquet. It smelled, as everything did, like fresh house paint.

"Whatcha got?" Metelis asked as he sat down across from me. He studied the sketches I'd spread on the floor and pulled at his long-suffering ears.

"Just some papers I found," I said. One of the advantages of being a mysterious boarder was not having to explain things too clearly.

Metelis nodded sagely, used as he was to my nonanswers. "Looks like the artist got better as he went along," he said, reading the sequence backward.

"Looks like."

"Heard you had company for breakfast."

"Did you?"

"Actually, I seated her myself," Metelis said. "That's how I knew she was waiting for you. She asked for you by name. I told her yes, Owen Keane, third-floor penthouse, our star tenant."

I smiled, not at the compliment, but at the confirmation that Diana had been there specifically to contact me.

"She's a star tenant herself," Metelis continued. "She's taken the best rental Glass Realty had. The Coryell place, two blocks south on Ocean Avenue. White stucco single story. Only about twenty years old. Solid as they come. Two baths, both ceramic. Hardwood floors. Tile roof. Air-conditioned."

Being a career renovator, Metelis was obsessed with house features. It was just my luck, I thought, to stumble onto a connection to the local gossip network and get nothing from it but plumbing specifications. But his next offering was more interesting.

"Paid cash for it," he said. "Rent and deposit. That's all she's used in the month she's been here. Cash. No credit cards. No checks."

No records, I thought, and no way for anyone to trace her to Spring Lake.

"What's she do for a living?" Metelis asked.

"She didn't say." I was rescued from the challenge of further vagueness by the arrival of two more of the Gascony's sunburned guests. Metelis went off to get them their cardboard wine. I folded Harry's sketches and retreated into the cool interior of the house.

My initial impulse on hearing my landlord's story had been to contact Father Peter to learn something specific about Diana Lord and her balked wedding. I shook that thought off as I entered the house. Mr. Ohlman wasn't paying me to chase after mysterious women. Actually, that reservation had very little stopping power. What really made me reconsider was the idea of facing little Amanda and explaining to her why I'd let myself be distracted from my job.

I finished my wine in the Gascony's dusty living room while I read through the accident reports. That process left me depressed and lonely. I flipped through a large scrapbook that Metelis had filled with local restaurant reviews and menus and picked a quiet-sounding place for dinner, the Solstice, in nearby Sea Girt.

The Solstice occupied an old beachside house that was pleasantly dilapidated. My table was in a screened side porch. There I drank wine from a real bottle and watched as a young boy on the beach launched a kite into the offshore breeze. It ran upward in the steady wind as mechanically as a flag being raised on a pole, and it stood against the darkening blue like a photograph of a kite superimposed on the changing seascape. After a few minutes, the boy reeled the kite in, feeling, perhaps, that there was no challenge to the exercise and no point. That was how I was feeling, at least.

It was dark when I got back to Spring Lake. I drove slowly around the lake with my window rolled down. From across the still, black water came the sound of a clarinet. This was one other part of Harry's routine that I'd been able to identify. Every night at sunset he played for an hour or so. It gave me an easy way of checking in on him. For the second time that day I thought of Boston College. This time the memory was

of evenings when Harry, having had one beer too
many, would sit at the open window of our dorm room
and play his clarinet until the resident assistant, a burly
graduate student from Ireland, came and took it away
from him. Harry was now playing a blue, nameless
piece I remembered from those days, repeating one
phrase again and again as though he was trying to play
it perfectly. I left him to his work and drove back to
the Gascony to read myself to sleep.

I WAS AWAKENED before dawn by the sound of a
floorboard creaking quite near my bed. I opened my
eyes, but my head refused to turn toward the sound. I
lay stiffly, listening for an echo. In the phony moon-
light of a nearby streetlamp, the gauze curtains at my
window moved rhythmically in and out, creating the
illusion that they were swaying in response to the soft
crashing of the ocean. I forced myself to roll over.
There at the foot of my bed was Diana Lord, dressed
as I had first seen her, in a tee shirt and bathing suit.

"Snuck up on you," she said.

I didn't answer. I was waiting for my heart to slow
to something like a normal rate. It promised to be a
long wait. I pushed myself up into a sitting position,
raking my head across the carved headboard in the
process. That awkwardness drew no response from
Diana. She interpreted my retreat as an invitation to
sit down, and she did so, moving with slow ease to a
point on the side of the bed very close to me.

"I told you I'd be back," she said.

I could now see that her tousled hair was wet. It gave
me an opening which I used to express my disorienta-
tion in a series of questions. "Have you been swimming?" I asked.

"Yes," she said.

"In the ocean?"

"In the lake."

"That's illegal, isn't it?"

Diana shrugged, extending one shoulder through the neck of her shirt. "I swim every night. I always have. The lake is as good a place as any."

It occurred to me that this was my chance to learn something of Diana's secret, but that thought had to compete for my attention with the memory of Shelly's warning that Diana could be trouble. In the end, my curiosity won out. "You wanted to ask me something this morning," I said. "Were you wanting my help?"

"Are you available?"

"I'm working on a job now," I said.

"A job?"

"I was sent here to look after someone. A friend."

Her left hand settled softly on my knee. "What are you, a guardian angel?"

"Something like that."

"Who sent you?" she asked.

"His father."

"Who art in heaven?"

"Who art in Massachusetts," I said.

Diana released my knee and ran her fingers lightly up my thigh. "You don't feel like an angel," she said.

I would have agreed with her, had I still been able to speak.

Diana leaned toward me slowly, until her lips were close enough for me to feel her next line. "A guardian angel is exactly what I need," she said.

What followed was enough like a dream to make me wonder if I had really awakened. That quality was due

in part to Diana, as beautiful and unreal as any dream.
Her skin was still cool from her swim, and she moved
with the noiseless grace of an apparition. Or perhaps
the dream quality came from the shock of watching a
long-lost fantasy come true. *Keane meets girl at the
shore on a soft July night* was a scenario I'd dreamt of
as a boy. In those innocent imaginings, the beautiful,
elusive woman had been an unattainable ideal, the
bearer of a forbidden knowledge. That was another
link to Diana. I held her tightly now, but not her secret.

When I woke again just before dawn, I was alone. I
crossed the creaking floor to the door of my room and
tried the knob. The door was locked.

SEVEN

LATER THAT MORNING, Shelly breezed past my table in the Gascony's dining room balancing two loaded plates on each extended arm. "Telephone for you," she said briefly.

I took the call in the nook off the dining room that George Metelis used as an office. The caller was Harold Ohlman, Sr.

"Owen," he said. "I've good news. The Nickelsons can see you today at noon. Is that a problem? They're the friends of Harry and Mary who had them over that last night. Do you know them?"

"No," I said, "I don't. Noon's no problem. What's their address?" I wrote it down on an official Gascony Inn pad. The nook was lit by a single stained-glass window that cast a checkerboard rainbow across the desk top and my moving hand.

"There's one more thing," Mr. Ohlman said. "I've arranged for you to speak with Mitchel Henry. Recognize that name?"

"Yes," I said. Henry was the other driver from the accident. "How did you manage that?"

Mr. Ohlman sounded pleased with himself. "I spoke with his attorney, a public defender named Charles Smith. He's anxious to cooperate in the hope we'll support a minimum sentence. I didn't promise him anything. Don't you either."

"I won't."

"Go easy on the Nickelsons," Mr. Ohlman added. "They're nervous about the liability angle. Don't scare them."

"I won't," I said again.

"Now, what have you got for me? Anything interesting happening there?"

Diana Lord's midnight visit certainly qualified, but I wasn't in the mood to raise Mr. Ohlman's blood pressure. "Harry sketched for a while yesterday," I said. "It seemed to upset him." It upset his father, too, and he made a noise like an angry horse. I remembered then that Mr. Ohlman had a poor opinion of his son's artistic side. "Harry didn't take his morning walk again today," I added. "I don't know what that means."

Mr. Ohlman was curt in his disappointment. "Find out," he said. He hung up the phone before I could answer.

At ten o'clock I was heading north on the Garden State Parkway, thinking of Diana Lord. Her visit seemed even more dreamlike now against the dreary background of the midmorning traffic. Dreamlike and disturbing. Mr. Ohlman's call had seemed timed to increase the guilt I was feeling over my divided attention. On the positive side, the call had also given me a way of making amends. I had set out to follow up this lead without my usual vacillation. If nothing else, I thought, the trip would get me out of Spring Lake for the day and out of the range of Diana Lord's attraction.

To exorcise her from my thoughts, I reviewed the facts I'd gleaned from my time with the accident reports the previous afternoon. The accident had occurred at one o'clock on a Sunday morning in a light freezing drizzle. The Ohlmans' BMW had been traveling east on Cold Springs Road, which had also been called State Road 617 on the state police report. They had arrived at the intersection with the Randolph Pike, State Road 656, and, having the green light, started across. Halfway through the intersection, they were struck almost broadside by a pickup that had run the red light on the Pike. Mary was killed instantly, and Harry was badly hurt. According to witnesses, the driver of the pickup, Mitchel Henry, had never even slowed down. Remarkably and unfairly, Henry escaped with only cuts and bruises. His blood alcohol level had tested at .19, nearly twice New Jersey's legal limit.

I followed the Parkway north until I came to Interstate 78. I went west on 78 for a short time in heavy, aggressive traffic. Then I stepped down several grades to State Highway 27, which took me into Morristown itself. That town had been Harry's compromise between a prestigious address and a reasonable commute to his office in New York City. The Ohlmans' home was actually in Cream Ridge, a western suburb. I drove through Morristown and past Cream Ridge without stopping. I was a few minutes ahead of schedule, and it occurred to me that I could use the time to visit Mary's grave. I decided instead to visit the spot where she'd died.

The Nickelsons lived a dozen miles west of Morristown on Cold Springs Road. When I reached the Randolph Pike intersection, I pulled into a former filling station that was now either a very large vegetable stand or a tiny farmers market. I left the Chevy for a moment and walked to the edge of the intersection. Without the shore breeze I'd grown used to, the air seemed heavy and moist. Like many of the secondary roads in the northern part of the state, the two that met here were winding and narrow. They could easily have been descendants of colonial roads or even earlier trails. The two roads crossed at an odd angle at a point that was, for Cold Springs Road, the bottom of a long, curving descent. The cockeyed layout of the intersection made me devalue one theory I'd been forming: the idea that Harry might be blaming himself for failing to spot the oncoming car.

The Nickelsons' home was a barn-sized colonial on a small lot in a development called Washington's Rest. I pulled in next to a Mercedes, whose engine was still making ticking sounds. Frank Nickelson came to the front door before I had a chance to ring the bell. My noontime appointment had been selected to coincide with his lunch hour.

Nickelson was about five ten and trim with oversized eyeglasses and a haircut that was ten years too young for him. His handshake was firm and prolonged. "Harry's dad said you were looking into the accident for the family," he said. "We're glad to help. Mary was a good friend. A really good friend. This is my wife, Angela."

I'd heard that married people begin to look alike after a time. It was certainly true of the Nickelsons. Mrs. Nickelson wore the same type of oversized plastic glasses as her husband. She also had the same sandy brown hair, which she wore in a short, choppy style. "How's Harry?" she asked.

Her concern sounded genuine, and I almost gave her my opinion. Instead, I fell back on empty honesty. "I don't know," I said.

They led me into a dark living room decorated in a hunting motif. The walls were dotted with old prints showing horses, riderless and mounted, and dogs, singly and in packs. The brass candlesticks on the low table that separated my chair from their sofa were shaped like miniature hunting horns.

I took out a prop notebook and pretended to review my notes. The page I'd opened to actually contained an accounting of my meals for the last week. "How well did you know the Ohlmans?" I asked.

"We're old friends," Mr. Nickelson said.

"We go back four or five years," his wife added in smiling contradiction.

"You met socially?"

"Mary and I worked together on a school board committee," Mrs. Nickelson said. Mr. Nickelson put a hand on hers.

"On the night of the accident, the Ohlmans were your guests for dinner. Is that right?"

"Yes," Nickelson said. His wife nodded solemnly.

"How did they seem to you that evening?"

"What do you mean?" Nickelson asked.

"Were they upset about anything? Did they seem tired or worried?"

"No," Mrs. Nickelson said. "We had a very nice time. Mary was very relaxed. Happy. Harry was..." she paused, searching for a word.

"Fine," her husband said. "Harry was never the life of the party. He was quieter. That never meant anything."

I wondered for a moment what it actually might have meant, remembering parties that Harry had enlivened considerably. Probably just that Harry had been bored. It was easy to picture him on the sofa be-

fore me, listening to Mary and Angela reorganize the
school board or Nickelson discuss fox hunting, wishing he were somewhere else.

I'd come to the first of my delicate questions. "Did
Harry have much to drink that night?"

Again Mrs. Nickelson spoke first. "No," she said
emphatically. This time I saw her husband squeeze her
hand.

"We had a drink and then some wine with dinner,"
Nickelson said. "Harry barely touched the wine.
There's never been any suggestion that he was drunk,"
he reminded me. "The police looked into that."

I nodded in agreement and stared at my phony notes
while I phrased the next question. It had the potential
to set the local gossip mill on overtime, but I couldn't
help that. "I'd like to ask one thing in the strictest
confidence," I began. "Do either of you have any
reason to believe that Harry has ever used drugs?"

The Nickelsons stared at me for a moment. The
square panes of their twin eyeglasses were each reflecting an image of a picture window behind me. The
four bright squares that resulted now looked like a
touch added by a cartoonist to complete a caricature
of shocked amazement.

"Absolutely not," Nickelson finally said. "The
Ohlmans were the last people who would be involved
in anything like that."

I silently agreed with him. I was content to leave it
at that, but my host was not.

"This isn't the kind of area where that sort of thing
goes on," he said, growing more offended with each
word. "The idea that all people who have attained a
certain level of financial success are sitting around

snorting their brains out is a television fantasy. An insulting, vicious stereotype."

This time it was Mrs. Nickelson who did the hand squeezing. Her husband stopped speaking abruptly, as though his plug had been kicked out of the wall socket.

"Mary wouldn't have put up with anything like that," Mrs. Nickelson said. "She didn't even like taking medicine. When her daughter was born, she had a spinal block to avoid drugs. Her doctor fouled it up, and she had chronic back pain after that, but she was too stubborn to take the pain-killers they gave her."

I thanked the Nickelsons for their time and left them to eat their lunch in peace. I ate mine in a café called Bart's a block from the Morris County courthouse in Morristown. Bart's was refreshingly out of step with the ye-olde-colonial flavor of the area, being an unreformed greasy spoon, founded—as its sign proudly proclaimed—in postcolonial 1945. As the single waitress poured coffee into my mug, whose surface was as gray and pitted as an old soup bone, I inquired about the Washington connection.

"Did George sleep around here or what?" I asked.

She fired off a reproving snap with her gum. I thought for a moment she was going to ask "George who?" Instead, she replied: "Washington brought his army here after winning the Battle of Princeton in January 1777. We think he slept a lot that winter." Having remedied that deficiency in my education, she moved on down the counter.

Perhaps it was because I was coming off a series of minor defeats and not a victory, but I had no desire to linger as Washington had in Morristown. I was early for my rendezvous with Mitchel Henry's public defender, Charles Smith.

Smith was early, too. Mr. Ohlman had described Smith as anxious, but that adjective seemed totally wrong for the person I found waiting for me on the courthouse steps. He was a young man with physical qualities that gave him the dignity of age, which is a nice way of saying that he was stout and losing his hair. Part of his dignity came from his deliberate manner. I held my hand out ready to shake his for several seconds while he slowly shifted the books and papers he carried. At the same time, he began to speak, sounding like a man who had just been roused from a deep sleep.

"Mr. Henry is something of a problem," Smith said. "I gather he has been all his life. First to his parents. Then to the school system. Now to me. He's a resentful young man. Angry, as they say."

As we climbed the courthouse steps, Smith added: "I don't know what you're expecting from him. I hope it's not too much."

What I was looking for from Mitchel Henry was the same thing I had been searching for unsuccessfully all day: some contradicting fact that would color the black and white of the accident reports. Some detail that would tell against my friend Harry and justify the guilt Father Peter had recognized. Henry was the last stop along this line of inquiry.

As the setting for our interview, I'd envisioned a large gray room and a wall of wire-mesh windows with prisoners on one side and their weeping relations on the other. Smith led me instead to a pleasant conference room with wooden furniture and padded seats. Mitchel Henry arrived a few minutes later in the company of a single deputy, who towered above him. In addition to being short, Henry was slight. His small stature was one of the reasons he looked younger than his actual age, which I knew from the accident reports to be twenty-three. His skin was pale, and the hair on his chin and upper lip was long and thin. So was the oily brown hair on his head. His eyes never opened more than halfway, and they looked straight at me with no apparent emotion.

I was having a hard time controlling my own emotions. My heart had begun to beat faster during our wait for Henry, and my palms were leaving moist outlines on the shiny tabletop. I'd previously been able to think of Mary's death as an accident, something terrible and pointless, but also random and unintentional. Henry represented the darker possibility that Mary had died because one unhappy man had lashed out carelessly at the world and taken her life as his revenge.

I made an effort to slow my breathing while Smith introduced me and Henry lit a cigarette. When Smith had finished, I said, "Describe the accident."

Henry took a long drag on his cigarette. The smoke came out at me as he answered. "Got drunk doing shots at the Red Sky in Mount Freedom. Got throwed out. Don't remember the rest."

My next question came out on its own, gray and spent like Henry's cigarette smoke. "Are you sorry?"

"Hell yes," Henry said. "I'm sorry I can't get me another fucking drink."

I stood up too quickly for the guard's liking. He took a step toward me and then froze with his hands

held slightly away from his sides. Smith was looking
down at his pile of books. Henry was considering the
burning tip of his cigarette. After a moment, I stepped
from the tableau and started back to Spring Lake.

EIGHT

I DIDN'T ESCAPE the humid heat of Morris County by driving back to the shore. It was waiting for me in Spring Lake, piled up above my head in rolling gray clouds. The storm broke just after dark. From the shelter of the bathing pavilion, I watched as the curving shoreline was lit by one blue bolt after another. In each flash, the restless seascape was frozen for a second like a giant photograph. After the fireworks died down, the rain settled into a steady, easy pace that continued throughout the night.

When I awoke, alone, on Friday morning, the rain was still falling. I rolled over and slept in until ten o'clock. Then, as a penance, I called Father Peter to report my lack of progress.

His good humor was unaffected by the weather. "I've arranged to visit with Harry at one," Peter said. "Come by at two and we'll compare notes. Bring your car."

At one o'clock I was back in my third-floor room, setting my expensive camera on its tripod. The sun had just broken through, which meant that the humidity would shortly be climbing as the rainwater burned off. For the moment, however, the air was clear of haze. St. Brigid's and the southern third of the lake were blocked from my view by houses and trees. I didn't pick up Father Peter in my telephoto lens until he was halfway to Harry's cottage. He was in uniform today, at least the summer version: black pants and short-

sleeve black shirt with Roman collar. His pace was
brisk, and he pumped his arms in the fashion of the
aerobic walkers I'd observed while following Harry.

Harry came out of the front door of his cottage as
the priest turned onto the front walk. It was my first
glimpse of Harry since he'd torn up his sketches on the
boardwalk two days before. He looked disheveled and
disoriented. He held one hand up to shield his eyes
from the sun as he looked about at the day. I focused
on him, and, when he lowered his hand, I pressed the
shutter release and advanced the film. I expected
Harry to lead Father Peter back into his cottage, but,
instead, he followed the priest down the front walk
toward the lake.

The two men crossed Lake Shore Drive and headed
south along a lake bank whose wet grass shimmered in
the sun. Harry was walking well, I was pleased to see,
with only a trace of his limp. His head was bent forward as he listened to the shorter man speak. That
Father Peter was doing all the talking was obvious
from his enthusiastic gestures. I couldn't interpret
them, even with the aid of the powerful lens. He might
have been explaining the Trinity or just telling Harry
about an especially crisp nine iron he'd hit that morning. I watched them walk south until my view was
blocked.

Then, instead of calling it quits, I swung the camera back along the lake shore to the north. On the
wooded northern tip of the lake, I saw a single figure
walking with long, unhurried strides. Diana Lord. She
was carrying a small shopping bag in one hand and
looking straight ahead in her indifferent way. When
she was clear of the shade of the trees, she raised her
face toward the blue sky and, coincidentally, toward

me. I snapped two quick pictures before she looked away. Mr. Ohlman could sue me later.

I realized then that Diana would probably pass the Gascony on her way to Ocean Avenue. Without a thought of Harry, I deserted my post and descended to the front porch of the house. The painters had packed up and moved on, and the porch had reacquired its heavy wicker furniture. I sat down in an oversized rocker and picked up a newspaper, intending to let Diana surprise me again. That strategy lasted all of a minute, undermined by the fear that she would amble past in her melancholy cloud and not see me. I abandoned the rocker and the newspaper and set off down the front walk to meet her.

My timing was accidently perfect; Diana was one house away when I reached the end of the Gascony's walk. She was barefoot now, carrying her sandals as a counterweight to her sack. Her smile of greeting softened the dark look of her eyes.

"Hello, Clarence," she said as she came up to me.

"Owen," I said.

"I gave you an angel name," Diana said. "You're an angel, right?"

"Right," I said.

"Have you been watching over me?"

I may have blushed at that question, as it reminded me of my nearby Nikon. "I've been thinking about you," I admitted.

"That's even better," she said. "Come by tonight. I want to talk with you."

"What time?" I asked. "Midnight?"

Diana didn't blush at that, but she did smile. "Nine," she said. "214 Ocean Avenue." She then strode off without a backward glance, a fact I confirmed by watching her until she disappeared around the corner.

NINE

AT TWO O'CLOCK I drove to St. Brigid's as ordered. Father Peter was waiting for me on the rectory steps with two large boxes.

"Good man," he said in greeting. "You don't mind if we run a couple of errands while we talk, I hope. My car is in the shop. We won't be gone more than an hour, I promise."

"Okay by me," I said.

"Go out to Ocean Avenue," Peter said after we'd loaded the boxes, "and head south toward Sea Girt. You mentioned on the phone that you'd looked into the accident. I take it that didn't pan out."

"No," I said. "The police reports were pretty straightforward. The only thing Harry can be accused of regarding the accident is bad timing. He hadn't been drinking much, according to the couple who entertained the Ohlmans that night."

"You spoke with them?"

"Yes."

"Did you happen to broach the subject of drugs?"

"Yes," I said. "They never heard the word before. The husband's reaction was violent enough to justify a urine test. But the wife told me something—reminded me of it, actually—that makes me discount drugs as a factor in the accident. Mary was a little bit of a health nut. She didn't like Harry to smoke a cigarette or drink a scotch and water. She wouldn't take an aspirin herself if she could help it."

"You knew that about her?" Peter asked.

"Yes," I said.

"Just how well did you now Mary Ohlman?"

I slowed to let a sunburned family cross Ocean Avenue in safety. "Since you've spoken with Harold Ohlman, Sr., you already know the answer to that," I said.

"He mentioned that you and Mary dated in college. He didn't say why you broke up. Was it Harry?"

"It was the priesthood," I said.

Peter smiled and nodded, as though I'd told him something he'd expected to hear. "I see. Sorry to get us off the subject. Go on with your report."

"There isn't much else. I met the other driver from the accident."

"You told me he was in jail."

"That's where I met him." I didn't add anything, unable to put my opinion of Mitchel Henry into words.

"That bad?" Peter asked after we'd driven a block in silence.

"Yes," I said. "I don't understand how Harry can be blaming himself when that creep's available."

"Pull into that lot next to the fire station. We share bingo equipment with these folks. I figure it will get us priority service if the church ever goes up."

We carried the boxes into a dark, cool hall attached to the firehouse. Inside, two men in blue uniforms were setting up folding tables. They waved to Father Peter without speaking.

"I'm sorry I sent you on a wild goose chase, Owen," Father Peter said. We set the boxes down on a low platform that ran across one end of the room. "I was hoping you'd find something to explain the guilt that's eating at Harry. Of course you realize that just because Harry wasn't using drugs when Mary was alive doesn't mean he isn't using them now."

"I know. How was he today?"

"No better. A little worse, maybe. Less open with me. Less interested in general. I tried out a new sermon idea on our friend. The subject is 'Letting Go.' The gist of it is that we can never be happy in this life until we learn to let go." In the empty hall, the priest's voice took on a theatrical quality. I decided that he was rehearsing again, with me and the two firemen as the congregation. "We have to let go of the things that hold us back. The injuries, the insults, the regrets, the failures. Even the memory of a loved one can be something that weights us down."

I must have started to squirm in my imaginary pew. Peter's voice dropped back to a normal level. "What's the matter?" he asked. "You're looking like a hard sell."

"Sorry," I said. "I just think that telling Harry Ohlman to let go of his feelings about Mary is like telling a drowning man to swim. If he knew how to swim he wouldn't be drowning."

"I hope it's more like telling people to learn to swim before they get in too deep. Harry is an exceptional case."

"He's the exception I'm interested in," I said.

Peter looked at his watch. "We'd better be on our way to the next stop." When we were back in the car, he said, "Head north on Ocean and turn left at the first light. I have to visit a parishioner in the county hospital. It's inland on Route 71."

We rode in silence for a time. I decided that the priest had nothing further to tell me about Harry, so I changed the subject.

"That young woman who's been coming to you for instruction," I began.

"Diana Lord."

"Yes. Have you made any progress with her troubles?"

"I've never really defined them," Peter replied. "She won't tell me any more about this wedding she's run away from. I'm more concerned now about something else. She seems to be preoccupied with death. I have no idea why. Do you remember that story I told you about Brigid Kelly?"

"The girl who drowned in the lake?"

"Right. Diana is fascinated by that tale. She knows more about Brigid Kelly now than I do. As for her interest in the Catholic faith, I've come to believe that it's no more than superficial curiosity. She's really only interested in the oddities of the religion, in relics, for instance, and miracles. And of course the subjects that touch on this fascination of hers: the Church's view on death, the afterlife, purgatory, suicide, et cetera. Yesterday she stopped in to ask about angels."

I looked over to see if the priest was waiting for my reaction. He was innocently examining the scenery. "What did you tell her?" I asked.

"I said to watch out for them. The angels in the Bible weren't sweet cherubs or Hollywood leading men. They usually meant trouble.

"What's your interest in Diana, Owen? If it's social, I think you could find a less complicated diversion. I have an idea that her canceled wedding and her melancholia are both by-products of an unhappy love affair. If she's already juggling two men, a third isn't going to be welcome."

I glanced at the priest as I checked traffic at a stop sign and noted that the scar on his forehead had darkened. "Diana has approached me," I said. "I think she wants my help."

"Your help?" the priest repeated in surprise. "What does she expect you to do for her?"

He was plainly irritated, and I remembered his earlier warning about his temper. I chose my next words carefully. "I don't know. She hasn't gotten around to telling me."

Peter stared straight ahead. "I'd be careful with this if I were you, Owen. It's one thing to play around with Harry's problem. You're a friend after all, and you have a stake. Diana Lord's something else entirely. You'd be out of your league. You could do some serious harm."

I already had an emotional stake in Diana Lord's mystery that Peter could know nothing about, as I had only begun to sense it myself. But it didn't seem like the moment to mention it. The priest obviously resented my involvement, so I decided to let the subject drop.

When we reached Route 71, Peter directed me to the hospital. I pulled up in a circular drive near the building's entrance. "Give me ten minutes," Peter said as he left me.

I got out of the car to stretch my legs on the brick plaza that fronted the building. There were busy highways on two sides of the grounds, and the rumble of truck traffic was constant. As I'd expected, the humidity had climbed steadily all afternoon. The horizon was now topped by a line of towering white

clouds that were climbing upward in another cycle of
heat and storm. As I paced, I tried to organize the information I'd gathered on Harry. The few facts were
all negative—he wasn't painting, he wasn't drinking,
he wasn't responsible for Mary's death—and I soon
grew discouraged. I mentally shifted my field of view,
reviewing instead the thin file on my other mystery,
Diana Lord. She had recently changed her mind about
getting married. She had money. She could mysteriously enter locked rooms. She was interested in
death—too interested, if Father Peter's insight was
correct. She was fascinated by the story of Brigid
Kelly. She swam every night in the very lake in which
Brigid had drowned.

My damp shirt suddenly felt cool against my back.
I was reminded of the two warnings I had received regarding Diana, Shelly's maternal advice that she was
trouble and Peter's blunt judgment that I was out of
my league.

The ensuing panic was interrupted by the sound of
the priest's rapid steps echoing off the bricks as he
strode across the place. "Let's go," he said. "I've got
a three o'clock meeting with the parish council."

I was hoping for a quiet drive back. I didn't get one.
Peter was restless as we pulled out of the hospital
drive. He shifted in his seat and tapped the various
parts of the Chevy's door with the knuckles of his
right hand, as though he were testing for a hidden
compartment. Finally, he turned to me and said, "I
wasn't telling you about that sermon earlier just to
hear myself talk. The idea of letting go has relevance
for you."

"What do you mean?" I asked, genuinely left behind by this new line.

"You told me when we first met that you were having problems dealing with Mary Ohlman's death. Problems that were getting in the way when you tried to help Harry."

I shrugged awkwardly in my shoulder belt. "Harry was driving the car that night. I know he wasn't responsible, but my emotions haven't caught on yet. I can't help resenting him for it."

Peter twisted around to face me. I had the feeling I'd stepped into a trap. "Your resentment of Harry has nothing to do with the accident," he said. "It has to do with your own unresolved feelings for his wife."

I pulled the car over onto the road's sandy shoulder with exaggerated care and put it into park. Then I turned to face the priest.

"You loved Mary," Peter was saying. "You gave her up because you thought you had a vocation. You failed at it. In the meantime, Mary married your friend. You've never been able to work any of it out, to let any of it go."

Peter was using his sermon delivery again. His voice seemed to bounce off the Chevy's square corners and hit me from all sides. "Mary Ohlman is the key to you and to this egotistical idea of yours that you can track down God the same clumsy way you've been following Harry Ohlman around. You can't put the seminary behind you like any other washout. You've got to prove that you're right and everybody else is crazy.

"But you know in your heart that you made a mistake, that you gave Mary up—turned your back on the only real grace in your life—for no good reason. There's your resentment of Harry Ohlman in a nutshell. You hate him for taking Mary away from you."

Peter ended his speech on a note of triumph, daring me to refute his analysis by sharing more secrets that he could turn against me. I choked down my anger instead, telling myself that this stranger had no special access to my heart.

I straightened in my seat and pulled the shift lever into drive. ''You'll be late for your meeting,'' I said.

TEN

THE HEAT OF THE DAY had collected in my rented room, absorbed by the flowered wallpaper and the ruffled curtains. I stayed there just long enough to change into my bathing suit. Then I set out for the beach, sans disguise and design. My run-in with Father Peter had left me feeling the way Harry had looked earlier that day, dazed and disoriented. I wanted to be alone for a while to think. Or to not think. I chose the cool isolation of the ocean over the hot emptiness of my room.

Ten steps past the beach entrance, I dropped my shirt and shoes onto the sand and broke into a run. Reenacting a memory of happier visits, I ran until the water was up to my knees and then dove into a wall of green that was poised to knock me down, cutting through it easily and frustrating its plan. I ducked under the next wave and the one after it like a boxer slipping in below an opponent's jabs. By that time, I was far enough out to ride the rounded backs of the waves without effort. I swam out as far as the lifeguards would allow and then treaded water. It was the nicest time of the day for the ocean, but most of the vacationers had already packed it in. I had this small piece of the Atlantic to myself, except for a few teenagers who were body surfing closer to shore and a lady in a fringed bathing cap who was swimming slow laps parallel to the beach.

My emotional reaction to Father Peter's outburst
should have been telling me something, but I was too
busy refuting his analysis to listen. It was easy enough
to answer one part of the priest's charges, the idea that
my strange preoccupations had somehow grown out
of the loss of Mary Ohlman. Mary herself would have
laughed at that notion and told Peter that my questioning had predated our relationship, that my search
had attracted, bemused, and ultimately disheartened
her.

At that moment, up to my neck in the Atlantic off
the Jersey coast, I was closer to the source of my quest
than Father Peter could possibly know. A few miles
south of Spring Lake was the town called Seaside
Park, where I'd once attended a retreat for high school
boys run by Brother Stephen Murawski, my Red Bank
friend, the retreat where I'd "found religion," in
Harry's words. As usual, Harry was wide of the mark.
I'd found my calling at the retreat, but it wasn't a religious one. I'd met a boy there who had turned the
days of prayer and discussion into a mystery by
claiming to have spoken with God. I'd cracked that
first case, but it had cracked me in turn, by revealing
the possibility of a godless universe. My wounds
weren't healed by the time I met Mary at Boston. They
hadn't healed yet.

It was so easy to deny the truth of Father Peter's
basic premise that I was encouraged to dismiss his
whole tirade, including the uncomfortable idea that I
might actually hate Harry Ohlman. I tried instead to
figure out what remark of mine had set off the priest's
sudden anger. It had been no single misstep, I finally
concluded. The trigger had been the idea that Diana
Lord had turned to me for help. That his anger was a

sign of professional jealousy was supported, I thought by the way he had trotted out my old failure in the seminary. But there was more going on behind the priest's anger than injured pride or some professional rivalry. In the end, I decided that Peter was genuinely concerned about Diana Lord. He was afraid that my interference could harm her.

As I started to swim in, I considered the idea that I should forget about my visit to Diana. I considered it seriously, knowing as I did so that I would go anyway.

LIKE ANY OTHER hopeful job applicant, I was prompt. At nine o'clock sharp I was on Diana Lord's rented front porch, pressing her rented doorbell. Her house was as my landlord had described it, a late fifties model thumbing its nose at its Victorian neighbors. It was a white stucco ranch with a green tile roof. The modest front lawn was also green, an achievement this close to the ocean. I looked around in the fading light and spotted the discreet heads of the automatic sprinkler system. White alyssum grew around the front porch in healthy clumps that reminded me of the afternoon's cumulus clouds. The scent of the tiny flowers was strong and sweet.

When Diana Lord first appeared on the other side of the screen door, her expression made me think that she had forgotten our appointment. A second later she was smiling at me like an old friend. "Hello, Clarence," she said, using the "angel" name she'd given me.

"Call me Owen," I said. "I'm off duty tonight."

"Good," she said.

She unlocked the screen door and held it open for me. Her perfume challenged the simple sweetness of the alyssum and shooed it back out the door.

I found myself in a large room with a tan tile floor. There was a rectangular rug in the center of the room. On two sides of the rug, a low-backed sofa and a love seat in matching white leather formed a right angle. At the corner where they met, an unstained oak table held a huge ceramic lamp with a dull finish. The sawtooth pattern that circled the lamp and the bright diamonds woven into the rug suggested the American Southwest. This motif was picked up by large prints that hung on the white walls. Their blue and purple designs looked like stylized mesas.

"Do the coyotes keep you up at night?" I asked.

Diana let that one pass and asked if I wanted some wine.

"Sure," I said.

I watched her go through an open doorway into a bright kitchen that was as bare and modern as the rest of the house. She was wearing a white shirt dress, cinched at the waist by a red belt. It was the most elaborate outfit I'd seen her in, and it made me think that she must have remembered our appointment after all. While she poured the wine, I looked around the place for some clues to the woman who rented it. There was little in the living room to distinguish it from a display area in an upscale furniture store. No books or magazines. No dishes or glasses. Only the package of cigarettes and the lighter on the end table suggested recent habitation. I casually examined the cigarettes. They were the same long thin brand that Diana had smoked on the Gascony porch.

Diana returned carrying two large wineglasses, whose pink contents seemed to glow in the white room. I tasted the wine and its sweetness brought back memories of ancient hangovers. It was Mateus, the wine of choice for important dates when I'd been a college student. When I'd been Diana's age. I drowned that unhappy thought in another swallow.

We sat on the leather couch, Diana with her back to the light. "How's your job going?" she asked as she lit a cigarette.

"Not very well, I'm afraid."

She blew a stream of smoke toward the ceiling. "What's the matter?"

That was a question I didn't care to think about, much less answer. For one thing, it reminded me of Father Peter's accusations from earlier in the day. But even without those echoes I would have dodged the question. I didn't want to feel guilty over my inability to help Harry. I wanted an escape, even if it opened the door to another unsolvable mystery.

"My mind keeps wandering," I said in reply to her question. "There's this young woman in town with a problem. She's right on the edge of asking for my help, but she can't bring herself to do it."

Diana didn't smile as I'd hoped she would. She sipped her wine. "Maybe she's waited too long," she said. "Maybe it's too late."

"Maybe. Why don't you tell me about it and we'll see."

"I thought you were off duty tonight."

"That was a joke. Angels are never off duty. It says 'We never sleep' on our business cards."

"I've watched you sleep," Diana reminded me. The statement also reminded her of something. She slid across the white leather that separated us and kissed me. It was a long kiss. My wine was warm by the time it was over.

"Come on," Diana said. She took my hand and stood up.

I remained seated. "Let's finish our talk first."

"Love first, then talk. That's our routine, remember?"

"I remember that we never get around to talking."

She squeezed my hand. "Are you complaining?"

"I want to help you."

"You are," she said. "You're helping me to forget."

She led me down a darkened hallway to a bedroom that contained evidence of premeditation. The bed's covers were pulled down, and a large candle burned on the night stand. She'd thought of everything except soft music. We had to make do with the slow steady bass of the ocean.

Later, as Diana lay with her head on my shoulder, I felt her shake slightly. I gently turned her face toward the light of the flickering candle. There were tears on her cheeks. I felt them fall on my shoulder as she turned away from the light. "What's the matter?" I asked.

"I'm scared," Diana said.

"Of what?"

She answered existentially. "Of things falling apart. Sometimes I just want to give up. Do you know what I mean?"

"I should," I said. "I've given up often enough."

"I mean giving everything up. Being gone. Being a memory."

"Like Brigid Kelly?"

Diana sat up, wiping at her tears with the back of her hand. "You know about Brigid?"

"I know she drowned in the lake."

"She died for love," Diana said solemnly. She seemed very young as she said it. I suddenly felt very old. "I mean, she lost her love and she couldn't live. Wouldn't it be beautiful to love that much?" It was a rhetorical question, fortunately. Diana was looking above and past me, staring into the darkness beyond the candle's light.

She broke the spell herself by sniffing loudly. "I'll be back," she said.

She disappeared down the dark hallway. I waited until I heard a door close quietly. At that cue, I stood up and felt my way to the wall switch. The room was almost as barren of personal effects as the living room had been. I searched it quickly. Diana's wardrobe consisted almost entirely of tee shirts and shorts. Two dresses, a windbreaker, and a faded blue robe hung in the closet. There was no purse or handbag to rifle. There was, however, a large portable stereo on the top of the dresser. It wasn't a new one, and it stood out in the impersonal, antiseptic room as it would have in a hospital. I lifted the stereo to look beneath it. As I tilted it, I noticed a round sticker that had been pasted on the top of the unit beneath its plastic handle. The sticker bore the blue and green emblem of a college. Drew University.

I was on my way back to the wall switch when I spotted my second clue. A tiny cardboard rectangle had been slipped into the frame of the dresser mirror. The card had once been white, but it was now soiled from handling. I recognized it as the type enclosed with flowers. On it was written in a bland copybook

hand: "Thanks. Love, Paul." I looked beyond the
card to the tanned face in the mirror. The poor guy
looking back at me didn't have idea one.

I left the lights on and got dressed. As I finished,
Diana appeared in the doorway, undressed and unself-conscious. "Are you going?" she asked.

"No," I said. "I want to have that talk. I think
clothes will help me concentrate."

She crossed to the closet and selected her robe. I sat
down on the side of the bed. She sat down on the floor
next to it and rested her head on my knee. "Forget the
talk," she said. "I don't want to cry again."

It was a tough argument to counter. When I didn't
say anything, she added, "Sorry I spoiled the evening."

"My fault. I was supposed to help you forget. I
didn't do a very good job."

"Some things are hard to forget," Diana said.

As so often happened, I was holding a weak hand
and hoping for a chance to play my one good card.
This seemed like the opening I needed. "Some people
are hard to forget," I said.

"Yes," Diana agreed softly.

"Like Paul, for example?"

She stood up quickly and backed away from the
bed. I saw that she was frightened, recognizing her
fear as it flashed before me like the lightning-lit seascape of the night before. Then the emotion was gone,
replaced by her old mask of indifference. "I think you
better go now," she said. When I didn't move, she
held her arm out stiffly and pointed to the door.
"Go!"

I walked through the house with Diana following a
few steps behind me. I intended to make a stand at the

front door, but I made the mistake of opening it first. Before I could turn around, she put her hands on my back and pushed me outside.

The push was largely ceremonial, and I understood its meaning. I walked away without looking back.

ELEVEN

THE NEXT DAY, Saturday, turned out to be one long roller coaster ride. It started slowly and innocently, as those rides often do. Harry appeared for his morning walk for the first time since he'd fallen on Tuesday. His strange smile was also back. My old friend looked altogether different than he had during my last visit to his cottage and during his talk with Father Peter. There was none of the shell-shocked sadness now. He was once again the Harry of Tuesday morning, happy and purposeful. I was unhappy and stuck for a plan.

As I padded along behind Harry, I was conscious of an embarrassing irony. I'd initially looked to Diana Lord's mystery as a break from my struggles with Harry's Gordian knot. Now I was grateful to Harry for reappearing to take my mind off Diana and our disastrous evening. Actually, Harry provided only a modest distraction. He maintained an easy pace on a shortened version of his usual course, and he paid no attention to me or to anyone else. My mind was free to wander. It wandered to Diana, of course. Despite my ultimate failure with her, I felt that I'd confirmed Father Peter's meager information. Her unhappiness did seem to come from an unsuccessful relationship. I didn't know whether Paul was her jilted fiancé or a third party. The sad, worn-out card from him suggested that, whatever part he had played in her life, he was now a memory. Diana had spoken of becoming a memory herself. I seemed to feel Diana's hopelessness again as I remembered Father Peter's prophecy that my meddling would end up harming her.

Harry led me back to the lake without an incident. I watched until he was safely across the bridge and inside his cottage. Then I returned to the Gascony.

Later, I sat in the inn's breakfast room at the table Diana Lord had used, pushing cornflakes from one side of my bowl to the other. I must have struck quite a contrast to the cheery eastern windows behind me. Shelly, the observant waitress, stopped by to comment on it.

"You look down," she said as she refilled my coffee cup. "Things going badly?"

"Nothing I can't handle," I said, dropping into the part I played for her, the sardonic private eye.

"It's the woman, isn't it?"

"It's always the woman."

The effort of holding in her "I told you so" was wrinkling Shelly's freckled brow. I decided to relieve the pressure. "You were right about her," I said. "If you see me straying again, shoot me in the leg."

She smiled and went off in search of half-empty coffee cups. Her place was taken almost immediately by her boss, George Metelis.

"Phone for you," Metelis said. "In your office."

Familiarity was working its magic on Metelis and me. He followed me to the little nook, whose stained-glass window was too bright this morning by half. I held the phone against my chest until my host remembered that he had more important business elsewhere.

The last person I wanted to talk with was Harold Ohlman. So it was no surprise when I heard his dry, supercilious voice on the line. "Did you enjoy your breakfast?" he asked.

My repartee with Shelly had left me primed for sarcasm. "My steak was underdone," I said. "How was yours?"

My employer was in no mood to fence. "I'm in New York," he said. "Mother and I came down for the weekend with Amanda. This afternoon I'm driving to Spring Lake. Alone. I'm going to have a talk with my son. I'm going to suggest that he come back to work, that he get on with his life. Suggest it firmly."

"I don't know if that's a good idea," I said. "I saw Harry this morning, I think he's settling down."

The receiver seemed to jump in my hand. "I don't want him settling down," Mr. Ohlman shouted. "Neither should you. You'll never learn anything at this rate. It's time somebody threw the deck in the air."

I didn't have enough of Mr. Ohlman's respect to hope to influence him. "What do you want me to do?" I asked.

"I want you to keep your eyes open. Let's act for a change and see what happens. I'll be there at four."

End of conversation. I hung up the phone with a feeling of impending disaster that made a short prelude of the morning and the early afternoon. A little before four, I donned my straw Bogart hat and black sunglasses and borrowed a newspaper from the Gascony lobby. I wandered down to the lake and took a seat on a shaded bench. There I pretended to read about the Tigers. Twenty minutes later, a Lincoln Town Car pulled up in front of Harry's cottage. Mr. Ohlman got out wearing a dark blue three-piece suit that was as out of place on this lazy Saturday as his grim expression. I caught a glimpse of Harry as he opened the front door of the cottage for his father. Then the two men disappeared inside.

Mr. Ohlman reappeared, alone, ten minutes later. Even from a distance I could see that his face was dark with anger. He held his arms stiffly at his sides, and his small hands were closed tightly in fists. He slammed the Lincoln's door shut behind him, and the car rocketed away from the curb a second later. Mr. Ohlman had fulfilled his mission and thrown the deck in the air. Now he was scurrying away before the first card hit the ground.

He barely made it. While the Lincoln was still in sight, Harry rushed out of his cottage, throwing open the screen door with such force that it slammed twice, once against the side of the house and then back against the door frame. His wild look confirmed my earlier judgment; his father's visit had destroyed the peace of the morning. Behind the quivering screen door, the front door to the house stood open. I was torn for a second between following Harry and searching his cottage again. But I knew I had to follow him. Mr. Ohlman's pressure was driving Harry to something. It was my unlucky job to discover what that something was.

Harry headed north toward the business district. His pace was rapid, exaggerating his limp. Until he was well past me, I sat on the bench with my newspaper held high. I deposited the paper in the first trash can I passed as I followed him across Lake Shore's hot, soft asphalt and up Main Street, I trailed Harry closely, closer than I'd ever done on our morning excursions, closer than you were supposed to. I wanted to see everything he did, to read the eyes of every person he passed. We were heading in the direction of the

liquor store with the neon shark's fin, but I didn't believe Harry would go there. I was thinking of the drug
angle again and feeling pretty sure about it. Harry had
the look of a man who needed a fix.

We joined a thin crowd of late-afternoon shoppers,
older, well-dressed couples and unescorted women of
various ages. None of them gave Harry a second look.
As he entered the block of tiny shops, Harry slowed
his pace and began to look around him, studying each
shop window he passed. I stopped to examine one
myself—a boutique whose window already displayed
the browns and grays of fall—to give Harry a little
more space. When I looked for him again, he was en-
tering a shop four doors away. I crossed Main Street
illegally and wandered north until I was across from
the store Harry had chosen, the Cashel House. It was
an Irish import shop, and its front window was cluttered with hats and sweaters and china and maps. I
couldn't see much of the inside of the store or anything of Harry.

I was standing in front of a travel agency. A cardboard cruise ship and a plastic airliner were on a col-
lision course in the agency's display case. I opened the
door and stepped into the quality air conditioning.
The room's only occupant was seated at a low wooden
desk holding a phone to his ear. He looked up at me
and smiled and went right on listening. That was fine
with me. I picked up a brochure on Bermuda and
stood by the front window. A long five minutes passed
while the gentleman at the desk said "uh huh" and
"exactly" over and over and I read about pink sand
beaches that I would never see.

Then the door to the Irish shop opened, and Harry
stepped out. He was smiling happily now, and he cra-

dled a package in one arm as though he were carrying a baby. He turned to his right and headed off in the direction of his cottage. I remained where I was, staring at the dark window of the Cashel House. The key to Harry's secret lay in that innocent little shop. I had only to cross the street to find it.

"May I help you?" the travel agent finally asked as I started for the door.

"I'll be back," I said, wishing as I said it that I would be, that I'd be back to book a trip far away from Spring Lake.

I walked up to the corner by the drug store and the fire station and recrossed Main at the light like a good citizen. My unhurried approach was part careful plan and part nerves. I felt a little light-headed in my excitement. I had the physical sensation of standing on the edge of a precipice. It was the moment when the roller coaster pauses at the edge of nothingness, the long last second before it falls away, although I didn't recognize it at the time.

I arrived at the Cashel House door, took a deep breath, and went in. The inside of the shop was as dark as the cluttered window had suggested. I took off my sunglasses and looked around.

The store was a single long room crowded with tables and display cases and, in the back, racks of clothes. The walls were crowded, too, with maps and posters of Ireland, Irish flags, and a large rack of coffee mugs decorated with Irish family names and coats of arms. Some energetic and monotonous fiddle music was coming from hidden speakers. The place was nothing like the opium den I'd been envisioning, and the lady behind the counter was no stock drug dealer. She was tiny, with silver gray hair and a complexion as pink as a baby's. She smiled at me in greeting, and I nodded, still wary and alert.

I began my tour of the premises, turning sideways to squeeze between tables piled high with cable-knit sweaters. I paused to examine a case of crystal. The intricately cut glass broke the sunlight that streamed through a ceiling dome into bits of yellow and blue and red that fell randomly across shelves of pewter and china. In the rear of the shop I walked slowly through racks of uncomfortable-looking woolen clothes. There were three doors on the back wall, two of which were ajar. Behind the first door was a dressing room no bigger than a closet. The second door opened onto a small office, filled to capacity by a single desk. The third door was closed and locked.

"That's our stock room," the lady behind the counter called out to me. "Can I help you find anything?"

Yes, I thought, a secret passage. Out loud I asked, "Do you sell tapes of that music?"

"Yes," she said. "I have them up here."

I retraced my steps to the front of the shop and briefly examined the cassette she handed me. "I'll take it," I said.

As she counted out my change, I tried another approach. "I thought I saw a friend of mine leaving your shop just now. I called to him, but he didn't answer me. His name is Harry Ohlman."

"Yes," the woman said, "it was Mr. Ohlman. He's staying here this summer. I see him every Sunday at the seven o'clock mass. I like the early mass. There's no singing, so it's a short service. Unless of course Father Marruca decides to lecture us on one of his causes. Last week it was the homeless people. The way he want on, I expected to meet half a dozen on my way home. He must see them on the golf course, poor man.

"I've never seen Mrs. Ohlman," she added. "She must not be an early riser."

"Harry's here alone," I said.

"Oh no. He's staying with his wife. My friend Helen Glass—we work on the altar committee together—told me that she rented the Ohlmans a cottage on the lake. The Bonning cottage. And Mr. Ohlman was just in here to buy a nice Waterford wineglass for his wife. Their pattern is Colleen, a very pretty one. He told me that he broke one of their wineglasses last winter. A wedding present, too. I said, 'It must have broken your heart.' So he bought a replacement today—so lucky I had it in stock—and he's going to surprise his wife with it tonight."

She ended her story with a happy smile on her face, but it slowly faded and her eyes grew wide. I realized then that I was staring at her in dumb amazement. I thanked her for her time and started for the door. Halfway there, I turned and asked where I could find Helen Glass.

"One block west of the light," the old woman said. "She owns the Spring Lake Motel."

A gingerbread Gothic house stood in the center of the Spring Lake Motel parking lot. The motel surrounded the house on three sides, its one-story wings suggesting open arms spread to gather up the house and pull it in. The house was the office for the surrounding motor court. Its other occupations were listed on neat signs that hung at intervals along the front porch roof: TAX PREPARATION, INSURANCE, NOTARY PUBLIC, REAL ESTATE, RENTALS.

There was only one office for all the businesses and only one person. Helen Glass wore her dark gray hair straight back from her face. Her well-tanned and wrinkled skin was marked here and there with dark, shiny spots, like leather freckles. She pushed herself back from a cluttered desk as I entered. "What can I do for you?" she asked.

I'd worked out my story on the walk over. "I'm interested in a rental cottage. You found one for some friends of mine. I'd like something similar."

She smiled and removed her glasses, letting them dangle from a golden chain that she wore around her neck. "Your friends are?"

"The Ohlmans."

She nodded. "The Bonning cottage. Harry and Mary. A very nice couple."

"You've met Mary?" I asked that question in a quiet voice, like a supplicant praying for a miracle at a shrine.

"I met her last summer when they stayed here for a week. Harry told me that his wife insisted they come back; she liked the place so well. I haven't spoken with Mary yet this year. I've meant to stop by, of course, to see if they needed anything, but I haven't had the time. This summer's been terrible. I should say 'wonderful,' but I'm getting too old to be this busy."

During her speech, I'd felt myself falling helplessly. Now I landed, sad and sick and feeling, irrationally, as though I'd lost Mary all over again. I turned without a word and left.

TWELVE

I WALKED AWAY FROM the Spring Lake Motel feeling omniscient, like the detective in the last scene of a movie. I understood things. I could see a pattern in the cracks of the old sidewalk I followed and a design in the bits of ragged cloud passing over my head. When I spotted the flat-roofed liquor store on the other side of the street, it seemed one more inevitable link in my chain. I interrupted my march to the sea long enough to buy a bottle of scotch from my old friend Tom. He slipped the bottle into a long, narrow paper bag, twisting the excess paper closed before he handed it to me. It was a sound precaution. Otherwise, I´might have had my first drink on the spot.

"Whatcha know?" Tom asked as he passed me my change.

"Everything," I answered. I did know everything. It was a gift I'd been given, the kind the gods in Greek mythology bestowed when they wanted to screw up somebody's life, the kind that comes with major strings attached.

When I reached the beach, I sat down on the sand. I set the bottle beside me and forgot it for the moment. The half-empty afternoon beach was the wrong setting for a denouement. I deserved a crowded drawing room, its doors guarded by burly policemen, and assembled in it an audience of principal characters who hung on my every word. Harold Ohlman, Sr., angry with me for stealing the spotlight but overawed by my knowledge. Father Peter, respectfully silent for a change. Harry, nervously looking for a way out. And Mary, dead Mary, alive again and renting a cottage in Spring Lake. She should have been the guest of honor.

For that was the secret I had uncovered. I'd solved a backward murder, like the backward detective I was. Harry hadn't killed his wife. His crime was not letting her die.

I recited the facts for myself as I might have done for a befuddled assistant. Harry Ohlman, in his grief, had come to Spring Lake, a place where he and Mary had been happy together the previous summer. Nothing unnatural in that. In Spring Lake, Harry had looked for comfort in the creative side of his nature. Still normal enough. Somehow he'd stumbled into a trap that lay waiting at the center of his creativity. I couldn't fault Mr. Ohlman for suspecting drugs. Harry's imagination had functioned like a drug, and, like a powerful pain-killer, it had turned out to have a destructive, addictive side. I'd learned all I needed to know about its dangers in Helen Glass's office. As she had matter-of-factly described Mary's presence in Spring Lake, I'd felt a second's irrational joy, as though we'd all been given a reprieve by heaven. Maybe it had started that innocently for Harry. Perhaps some stranger's misunderstanding had given him a brief relief from his pain, a relief he had decided to stretch out unnaturally.

My brilliant speculation was wasted on my dull-witted foil. I returned to a bare statement of the facts. Harry had begun to pretend that his wife was alive and with him in his cottage. That explained the smile that had so offended me. It explained why Harry wasn't drinking. It explained his reluctance to communicate

with his family and friends. Our sad, solicitous faces
would dispel the dream like the ocean breeze scatter-
ing a pretty cloud. Even little Amanda would remind
him. When his father had come today, unconsciously
throwing the fact of Mary's death in his son's face,
Harry had reacted like an animal flushed from its hole,
until the innocent interest of a shopkeeper had helped
him to reestablish his fantasy.

My discovery even explained Harry's punishment of
his barely healed leg. He ignored the pain on his
morning walks because the leg had never been broken, the accident had never happened. I remembered
then the morning when Harry had fallen a few yards
short of his cottage, the morning when he'd called out
Mary's name. I'd seen the moment as a demonstration of pain and grief, and I'd resented it, unfairly,
blaming Harry as I had been then. I now realized that
Harry had been calling out to someone he believed was
waiting for him behind the cottage door. Calling out
to the dream to help him fight off the reality of his
shattered leg.

The sand at my feet was dry and windblown and as
white and fine as the sand in a hotel ashtray. The
ocean must have thought so, too. Several cigarette filters were mixed in with the lighter bits of weed and
shell deposited by the last wave of the last high tide. I
collected those filters I could reach without standing
up. The nearest trash container was already playing
cornucopia for the local gull population. I dropped the
filters into my shirt pocket, as though they were val-
uable clues.

I was stalling, of course. Now that I held Harry's
secret, I didn't know what to do with it. I couldn't call
Harold Ohlman, Sr. He had no empathy for his son's

creative side and precious little sympathy for his grief. I couldn't leave Harry to his mercy. I thought of Father Peter, but our recent falling-out made me hesitate. Then I had a better idea, or what passed for one at that moment.

I went back to the Gascony and called Edward Hennix, a psychologist I'd met on an earlier case. Hennix ran a firm that specialized in discreet counseling for the employees of large, beneficent corporations. Those companies contracted with Hennix to provide confidential advice and assistance on drug, alcohol, and family problems, financial and legal matters, and anything else that might negatively impact an employee's productivity. It was the latest fringe benefit and the latest boom industry. While the Father Peters of this world struggled on alone in their crumbling rectories, Edward Hennix and his competitors stole their business with seven-day-a-week staffing and twenty-four-hour, toll-free hotlines.

Hennix's line was answered by a woman who recited the name of his firm: "Hand to Hand."

I asked for her boss.

"He isn't available at the moment," the woman replied. "I can connect you with another counselor."

"I don't need a counselor," I said, probably sounding to her exactly like everyone else who called. Before she could talk me into it, I gave her my name and the Gascony's number and hung up.

It was almost six o'clock. I felt I'd stalled as long as I could. I decided that I wouldn't wait for Hennix's advice. I would follow my original instinct of two weeks ago and talk with Harry, friend to friend. I'd failed at that before because I hadn't felt particularly friendly and because Harry hadn't opened up to me. Now he would have no choice.

THIRTEEN

HARRY WASN'T PLEASED to see me. I would have been disappointed if he had been. "Now what?" he asked in greeting. He had changed his clothes since his father's visit. His shaggy hair was still wet from the shower.

"Visiting day," I said as I stepped past him into the cool, stale air of his living room. "Your dad had the early shift. Now it's time for old friends."

"Dad called you, did he? Told you about his ultimatum, I suppose. Are you here to argue his case or to apologize for him?"

"Neither," I said. I sat down on the arm of the sofa and pulled the scotch I still carried from its paper wrapper. "I brought you a present. We're both going to need a drink."

Harry remained near the front door. "I have plenty," he said, pointing to the prop bottle that stood in the same spot on the mantel where I'd last seen it.

"No sense in making you redecorate," I said. I twisted the cap off my bottle and held it up. "Success to crime." Bogart's toast from the *Maltese Falcon* had been a favorite of ours at Boston. I drank from the bottle and held it out to Harry. He crossed the room to take it from me. Before drinking, he made an elaborate show of wiping the mouth of the bottle on his shirttail.

Harry handed the scotch back and sat down in the chair I had occupied on my last visit. I looked around the room. It was still orderly and impersonal. The only addition I could see was the crystal wineglass Harry had purchased at the Cashel House. It occupied a place of honor on the coffee table, waiting for Mary to discover it when she came home. I looked around for Harry's spotless ashtray and found it on the end table next to me. It reminded me of the castaway cigarette filters carefully stored in my pocket. I fished them out and dropped them into the clean blue circle of glass.

"That's better," I said. "I spotted that ashtray when I was here the last time. It should have bothered me, being cleaner than a holy water font."

"What do you mean?" Harry asked.

I took a drink and passed the bottle back before answering. "You've never been able to quit smoking for a month at a time. Not even with Mary bugging you. Why haven't you backslid now?"

Harry didn't bother to wipe the bottle this time. "You tell me," he said.

I realized that I would have to tell him, finally. He was never going to tell me. For the moment, I changed the subject. I pointed to the shining wineglass on the coffee table. "Pretty," I said.

"Yes," Harry agreed.

"Waterford, isn't it? Colleen, I think." I was stalling again with my phony expertise, and Harry knew it. He stared at me without answering.

I shrugged. "I want to help you, Harry. I owe you. Mary told me that once. Now it's payback time. You're in trouble. I know all about it. I'm the only one who has to know. But you've got to trust me." Something was wrong with my dull, flat delivery. I was trying to convey my friendship for Harry, but to my own ear I sounded like the reluctant hireling I'd been all along."

Harry seemed to sense the distinction. "You'd better get into your car and drive back to Red Bank," he said.

"There's no car at the curb, Harry. You should have noticed that. I walked here, and not from Red Bank. I have a room in Spring Lake. Over on Taylor Street. I've been here for almost two weeks now."

Harry's face had reddened. I could clearly see the veins standing out on his forehead. "You bastard," he said.

"There's nothing to be ashamed of," I said, pretending that Harry's emotion was something other than pure anger.

"You're the one who should be ashamed!" Harry fired back. "Sneaking around behind my back. What gives you the right to spy on me?"

There were any number of good answers to that. His father's commission gave me the right. The debt I owed Harry for saving me more than once gave me the right. I let those good reasons go and told him the truth. "Amanda asked me to look after you. She asked me to bring you back."

My answer checked Harry's growing anger. "Amanda?" he repeated, as though it was an effort to remember his daughter.

I charged into the small, quiet space her name had created. "Harry, what you're doing here is no good. It's dangerous for you. You may think you're in control. You may be now. But sooner or later you're going to lose touch."

We were both standing now, only a foot or two apart. "Mary is dead," I said. "She isn't in Spring

Lake. She isn't going to be. It hurts like hell, I know, but you've got to face it. You owe it to Amanda. You owe it to Mary.''

I should have been expecting the roundhouse right that Harry threw at me. It was an argument he'd used on me before. Maybe I was expecting it, since I caught it so expertly with the point of my chin.

The shock of Harry's blow was like a flash of blue that lit the inside of my head. I hit the carpet in a sitting position, but when I reached out to steady myself, it wasn't Harry's tired sculptured shag I felt. It was the worn grass of the Boston Commons. Harry was standing over me, young and moustached and wearing a work shirt and jeans. There was a cloudless blue sky above him where his ceiling should have been. Young Harry was yelling at me for something stupid I'd done, but I knew that wasn't the real reason he'd hit me. He'd knocked me down because he was jealous of Mary and me.

I opened my eyes. 1969 and the Boston Commons were gone. So was Harry. I was alone in his living room, which was lit by the soft light of early evening. There was a sensitive spot on the tip of my jaw that felt like a wad of gum stuck between the bone and the skin. When I'd mastered sitting upright, I got to my feet and made a slow tour of the cottage. There was no sign of my host.

The bottle of scotch sat undisturbed on the spot where Harry had set it down. I picked it up. My legs felt rubbery as I descended the front steps of the cottage. If there had been anyone watching, they would have attributed my weaving to the open bottle I carried. But my unsteadiness wasn't due to the scotch or even the sock on the jaw. I was worn out from my

roller coaster ride and drained by the blowup with
Harry. I was also feeling ashamed of myself. Harry
had been right about that. Father Peter had been right,
too. There was something standing between Harry and
me, some old unsettled score. Even I had been right on
one small point. I'd told Harry that it was payback
time. I just didn't know what I was trying to pay him
back for.

I sat down to rest and drink for a while in the woods
at the tip of the lake. I was also watching for Harry to
come back, hoping for a chance to undo some of the
damage I'd done. The chance never came.

I was good and drunk by the time I gave it up and
walked back to the Gascony. I made it to my room
unnoticed, intending to pack my bags for an early departure. Instead, I dropped onto the bed fully clothed.
I remember thinking as I closed my eyes that the day's
long ride was finally over.

I AWOKE WITH A START when someone touched my
hand. Diana Lord stood at the side of my bed, wearing the white dress of our last evening together. She
looked as frightened as I felt. It was dark, but I'd forgotten to pull down the shades, and the light from the
streetlamp wandered a few feet into the room. I could
clearly see Diana's eyes, incredibly large and lost. I
reached out for her hand, but she pulled back.

I judged from the advanced state of my hangover
that I'd slept for hours. The pain rang out in my head
as I struggled to raise it from the mattress.

"I came to say good-bye," Diana said. "I'm giving
up."

"Good-bye?" I repeated, still too groggy to com-
prehend. "Where are you going?"

"I don't know." Diana backed away from the bed as she spoke, growing indistinct in the darkness. "Maybe to be with Brigid."

She turned and ran from the room. I got up to follow her, moving with the frustrating slowness of a character in a nightmare. I could hear Diana running down the stairs as I reached the door of my room. The front door of the house slammed before I was halfway down the three creaking flights. She must have stumbled or hesitated as she left the house. When I came out onto the porch, she was still in sight, running down Taylor toward the lake.

My legs were finally waking up. I stretched them out in a steady stride, hoping to outlast her, but she never slowed down. The sycamore canopy smothered the streetlights. I ran through a tunnel of darkness with her white dress my faint, fading goal.

I called out to Diana as she crossed Lake Shore Drive. She turned back toward me and hesitated for a second, spotlit in the open road like a dancer on a bare stage. Then she disappeared into the shadows of the lake bank.

As I crossed the road, I spotted her on the wooden footbridge. She climbed onto the rail in a single effortless motion, as though she were being lifted by invisible hands. I called her name again as she dove into the black water.

FOURTEEN

I SAT ON THE GRASS at the edge of the lake, watching the water turn red and then gray, red and then gray. Behind me, the radio of the rescue truck hissed and crackled, the sound expanding hugely in the morning quiet. Occasionally, a voice broke through the static, asking some terse, garbled question. The men standing near me on the bank ignored the questions, so I ignored them, too.

Spring Lake was covered by a fine mist that floated a foot or two above the still, glassy surface. Here and there, white wisps descended from the mist to the water and swirled about in a secret breeze. It was the lake of my morning walks. That thought made me raise my eyes to Harry's cottage. All was quiet there. I knew that St. Brigid's would be visible to my left as a domed shadow, but I didn't turn my head to see it.

Somewhere beneath the still surface of the lake, two divers were at work. They were out some distance from the bank now, and I could no longer detect the small disturbance that their bubbles created on the perfect water. Near the footbridge, two firemen sat in a rowboat, smoking and waiting for the divers. The smoke from their cigarettes came through the mist to me, filling the morning emptiness as the sound of the radio did.

I felt the coolness of the morning through my clothes, which were still damp from my own futile attempt to find Diana Lord. I considered going back to the inn to change, but I knew I couldn't move from the spot where I sat, that I couldn't so much as stand up to stretch my legs. The men on the bank were ignoring me kindly, providing a private place for me with their averted eyes and muted voices. I hid gratefully in that sanctuary, invisible and helpless, knowing that my slightest movement would break the spell.

It was almost a relief, then, when a voice from the street above us broke into the silence. "Hey guys, could you knock off the flashers? We're going to have half the town down here in an hour as it is."

The speaker was a tall, heavyset woman who stood looking down at us from the top of the bank. She was dressed too formally for the early hour, in a navy blue suit and a white, high-collared blouse. She pointed down to me. "Come up and see me," she said.

I started up the bank. The newcomer looked out over my head to the rowboat and the divers, giving me a chance to examine her freely as I approached. I guessed her to be about my age; her curly brown hair was touched with gray, but her broad face was unlined. I noted that her shirt collar was fastened with an eccentric pin that looked like a child's doodle shaped in silver. The corner of a carefully folded white handkerchief stuck up an inch or so from the top of her jacket's breast pocket. Both the jacket and her pleated skirt looked freshly pressed.

Her brown eyes met mine as I stepped up to her, and she extended her hand. "You're Mr. Keane, I presume," she said. "My name is Pat O'Malia." She retrieved a small case from her suit coat pocket. I thought she was going to show me a badge, but instead, she handed me a business card. "I'm Spring

Lake's public safety director. That's sort of a cross between police chief and dogcatcher.''

When I didn't smile, she shrugged slightly. "You reported a possible suicide at three o'clock this morning. Would you like to tell me about that?''

I'd learned from earlier dealings with the police that they enjoy having people repeat themselves. For the third time that morning, I told the story of Diana's sudden appearance in my room and her dive into the lake. If the repetition had made my delivery stale, it didn't show in O'Malia's expression. She listened carefully and critically, her eyes narrowing in disbelief when I described Diana's fascination with Brigid Kelly.

"Amazing," she said. "That tale had long, gray whiskers when I was a girl. How could it have affected this Diana so much?''

"It must have reminded her of something," I said. "She came to Spring Lake to hide from some problem she was having. A wedding she wanted no part of.''

"More and more romantic. How well did you know this girl?''

"I only met her a few days ago," I said.

"And she was already stopping by your room in the wee small hours? You must clean up well.''

I'd had enough of O'Malia's cheerful humor. My hangover had been survived by a dull headache, and I was tired. Something terrible had happened, and it was all the more terrible for me because I couldn't begin to understand it. "I don't think this is a time for jokes," I said.

"Seems I've heard that before," O'Malia said amiably. "Tell me about Diana Lord.''

It was my turn to shrug. "She's sad. Confused. She's caught up in something that she can't handle alone. She admires someone who loved enough to die for love, which may just mean that she wants things to be that clear for her. She's young in some ways and old in others."

"Naive and world-weary at the same time?" O'Malia asked. "I'm afraid an all-points bulletin based on that description would net half the young people in the state. One side effect of growing up too fast seems to be never growing up completely. Kids today are like my darling husband's hamburgers, crusty on the outside and underdone on the inside."

As she spoke, O'Malia's eyes and attention wandered to the northern end of the lake. I turned to follow her glance and saw a white patrol car emerge from behind the grove of trees. "Belmar police," O'Malia said. "What do they think they're doing over here in the high-rent district?"

The white car stopped in front of Harry's cottage. After a minute or two, Harry climbed out of the car. He limped up the front walk without a backward glance and disappeared inside the house.

The patrol car circled the lake and approached us. "Busy morning," O'Malia said to herself. She waved at the car, and it pulled up to the curb next to us. "Running a cab service on the side, Frank?" she asked.

The man at the wheel wore a faded blue uniform. The deep lines in his brown face rearranged themselves as he smiled. "Just bringing back one of your high-class guests, name of Ohlman. He slept one off on our beach last night."

Owen Keane strikes again, I thought. I wanted to question the policeman about Harry, but I wasn't ready to admit another failure to O'Malia.

"Thought I could sneak in and out of the kingdom without Your Highness noticing," the smiling policeman said. "Should have known better."

"Damn right," O'Malia replied.

"What's going on here?" the policeman asked, looking beyond us to the lake.

"Rescue drill," O'Malia said. "Try to obey the posted speed limits on your way out of town."

The old policeman waved and pulled away, still smiling.

"Frank Capoletti," O'Malia said to me. "One of the best. Taught me how to break down a pistol when I was eight."

There was some activity on the lake behind us. The two divers had surfaced, and they were holding onto opposite sides of the rowboat, talking with the men inside it. After a long minute, one of the men in the boat looked up toward us and shook his head.

"No luck," O'Malia said. She put a hand on my shoulder. "You don't look very good, Mr. Keane. If I didn't know better, I'd say you ran that outfit through the Maytag while you were still in it." She pinched the material in my shirt. "I guess you're dry enough to be seated in one of our better restaurants. How about we get a cup of coffee while we talk?"

I said okay. O'Malia spoke briefly with a Spring Lake patrolman who had been standing a respectful distance away. Then she led me to a large Buick that was the same dark blue color as her suit.

As we pulled away from the curb, O'Malia tapped a number into her carphone. "Helen," she said into the handset. "This is Pat. Sorry about the early call. I knew you'd be up saying your morning rosary." She laughed at the reply. "Look, could you meet me at the Coryell place in half an hour? Bring your key. I'll explain when I see you."

As she hung up the phone, O'Malia said, "My people have been by the house already, of course. It's locked up tight, and no one answers the bell."

We were heading north on Main Street. As she drove, O'Malia looked over the fronts of the shops we passed like a general inspecting well turned-out troops. Half a block past the traffic light, she pulled into a parking space in front of a bakery. The interior of the shop was a long, narrow room divided lengthwise by a glass display case. The shop had just opened, and a young man in white was setting trays of donuts and rolls into the case. The shelves behind him were still empty. Along the wall opposite the counter was a line of small tables.

O'Malia greeted the three other customers by name. "Grab yourself a seat," she said to me. "I'll be right with you." She joined me a moment later, carrying two paper cups of coffee and two large croissants. She broke one of the rolls in half under her nose and inhaled. "Go ahead and try one," she said. "They're really good." When I didn't dig in, she added: "Breakfast is the best thing for a hangover."

"Who said I was hung over?"

"If you're not, your eyes got too much sun yesterday."

I must have smiled, because she said, "That's more like it. Eat something, and I'll tell you another one of my brilliant deductions, one that will cheer you up."

"What's that?" I asked.

"You don't believe that Diana Lord committed suicide. When I asked you to describe her back at the lake, you used the present tense. 'She's confused. She's sad.' You don't believe she's in the lake. Neither do I."

I chewed on the croissant and considered O'Malia's observation. She was right. I didn't believe Diana Lord was dead. I was still too numb to believe anything.

"Why did she dive off the bridge?" I asked.

"I don't know," O'Malia said. She wiped her fingers carefully on a tiny paper napkin. "But I promise you that I'm going to find out. In the meantime, tell me about yourself. What brings you to beautiful Spring Lake?"

I should have trusted O'Malia. I would have ordinarily. But that morning I wasn't dropping my left for anyone. I used the same lying technique on her that I'd employed earlier with Harry, slicing the truth so thin you could see though it. "I'm down here visiting an old friend. He's staying in Spring Lake this summer, getting over a loss. His wife was killed in an automobile accident a few months back."

I was expecting a token expression of sympathy, but O'Malia's brown eyes registered only curiosity. She managed to contain it, barely. "To think I used to know this place inside and out," she said.

"I was born here," she added, settling back in her chair. "My family goes way back in Spring Lake, as far back as the original building boom at the end of the last century. My grandfather was mayor here forever. He died in office when I was in high school. You heard Frank Capoletti call me 'Your Highness.' That's the way I felt myself when I was growing up, like I was a member of the ruling family. A few families really did run the town back then. Irish families. They're almost all gone now. It's getting harder to keep up with all the outsiders moving in." She smiled. "And harder to impress them with my reminiscences. We'd better get a move on. Helen Glass, the lady we're meeting, is another descendant of Spring Lake royalty. She doesn't like to be kept waiting."

O'Malia drove us by the lake on the way to the Coryell house. The patrolman O'Malia had left at the scene walked over as we slowed down. "Nothing yet," he said.

"So far so good," O'Malia said to me as we pulled away.

Helen Glass was waiting for us on Diana Lord's front step. She looked me up and down without pleasure as O'Malia and I followed the front walk, the flagstones of which were still glistening from the automatic sprinklers' morning shift.

"There's no answer to the doorbell," Mrs. Glass said. "What's this all about?"

O'Malia's reply sounded like a prepared speech. "I have reason to believe that your tenant may be hurt or in some difficulty. I'd like your permission to enter the house."

Helen Glass soaked that in for a moment. Then she said, "Hell," and turned to unlock the front door.

The Arizona living room looked less lived in than it had on my first visit, if that was possible.

"Wait here," O'Malia told us. She looked into the kitchen briefly. Then she followed the hallway into the back of the house.

We waited in silence for a few minutes. Then Mrs. Glass said, "Hell," again and marched off into the kitchen. A second later, I heard drawers opening and slamming shut, with an accompanying clatter of silverware.

O'Malia reappeared at the head of the hallway and signaled to me to join her. We stepped together into a gray bathroom lit only by the slivers of sunlight squeezing in between the Venetian blinds. There was a bath towel on the edge of the tub. O'Malia picked it up and held it out for me to feel. It was damp. She held the towel under her nose. Then she leaned over and sniffed at the damp collar of my shirt. "Helps to have the physical evidence following me around on the hoof," she said softly. "If this towel and your shirt weren't doused with the same lake water, I'll resign from the bloodhound society."

We returned to the hallway. Mrs. Glass was still banging around in the kitchen. "Have you been here before?" O'Malia asked.

"Yes," I said. "Once."

"What personal belongings did Diana Lord have?"

"Clothes," I said. "And a portable stereo."

"Follow me," O'Malia said. She led me to the bedroom where I had frightened Diana with my question about Paul. The stereo was gone. The closet and the drawers of the dresser were open and empty. I checked the dresser's mirror. The worn thank-you note was also missing.

"Someone's cleaned house," O'Malia said. "The question is, was it Diana Lord?"

Helen Glass now rejoined us, signaling her arrival with yet another "Hell." She took in the evidence of the room quickly. "Skipped by God," she said. "Skipped and left me holding a three-month lease." She turned on me angrily. "What's your part in all this? What were you doing in my office yesterday, pretending you know the Ohlmans?"

"The Ohlmans?" O'Malia repeated. "The Bonning cottage?"

"Yes," Mrs. Glass snapped. "He told me he wanted a rental like theirs. Then he turned on his heel and walked out, without so much as a 'kiss my ass.'"

"The same Ohlman we saw deposited on his doorstep this morning?" O'Malia asked me.

"Yes," I said. "The friend I'm visiting. The one I told you about."

O'Malia was confused, and she didn't like it. "You said his wife had been killed a few months ago."

"Oh no," Mrs. Glass interjected. "Mary's here in Spring Lake. Mr. Ohlman told me so himself."

It wasn't a room I would remember fondly. First I'd lost Diana's trust there. Now I was being ground between the truth and Harry's sad lie. "I'd like to speak with you alone," I said to O'Malia.

"I think that would be a good idea," she said. She consulted her watch. "It's quarter to eight. Be in my office at ten o'clock sharp. Be ready to tell me everything you know."

FIFTEEN

WHEN I REACHED the top step of my long climb up the Gascony's tower, I saw a piece of paper taped to the door of my room. I decided that it was my eviction notice and marveled at how quickly news traveled in a small town. The paper turned out to be a note from Shelly. Edward Hennix, the corporations' counselor, had called back. He'd left his home number.

For the first time, the old, formal bed in my room looked inviting, but I resisted the temptation to sleep. A shower and a change of clothes helped my resolve. I felt a little of the previous evening's anger returning, which helped, too. The anger wasn't directed at Harry now or at anyone but myself. I was tired of being a step behind the other players and tired of bumping my head as I groped around in the dark.

I didn't want to use the phone at the inn. I walked over to the boardwalk and used a pay phone in the shelter atop the bathing pavilion to call Edward Hennix. It was early on a Sunday morning, but O'Malia's deadline didn't allow me the luxury of waiting for office hours. I knew Hennix wouldn't mind. He was a less formal man than the degrees behind his name had once led me to expect. I'd learned a little about him since I'd made that misjudgment. Hennix had grown up in a Newark neighborhood that was as tough as New Jersey got. He'd worked his way through several colleges, intending to be a champion of the poor and oppressed. Instead, he'd ended up a well-paid businessman who solved the problems of the middle class. He felt guilty about this change of plans, but it didn't diminish the respect I felt for him. I admired anyone who could solve another's problems or simply cared enough to try.

"Keane," he replied to my hello. "What's that booming I hear?"

"The ocean. I'm calling from the beach."

"Damn," Hennix said. "You investigators know how to live. Let me guess: you're sitting in a lounge chair under a beach umbrella talking on a phone some sexy cocktail waitress carried out to you."

I glanced around the shelter. A teen wired into a pocket radio was sweeping up the cups and cans of the previous evening. The heavy wooden bench next to me was engraved with initials that went back generations. A green-headed fly on the scarred metal upright from which the phone box hung was eyeing me hungrily. "You guessed it," I said.

"So, what are you up to your neck in now?"

"I'm hoping you can tell me," I said. "I need your advice. It's a friend's problem."

"It's always a friend's problem," Hennix said.

"Right. This friend is a recent widower."

"How recent?"

"Five months. He's having trouble dealing with his wife's death."

"Loss of a spouse, they don't get any tougher," Hennix said. "It tops the list of stressors we use to evaluate a person's load. Widows and widowers carry a big one. They're more susceptible to illness, heart attack. They have a higher than average admission rate to mental hospitals. Did his wife die suddenly?"

"Yes."

"Worse still. What's this friend of yours doing? Drinking too much?"

"No."

"Drugs?"

"No," I said, embarrassed by Hennix's recounting of my own bad guesses. "He's pretending his wife is still alive."

Hennix whistled softly. "Pretending how?"

"He's staying in a shore resort where they spent a week last summer. He's supposed to be painting, but he's not. He's told one or two people that she's with him."

"Have you spoken to him?"

"Yes."

"Did he tell you that she's with him?"

"No," I said.

"Does he have any of her things? Clothes, jewelry?"

"No. I've looked through the place where he's staying. There was nothing like that."

"That's something positive. Have you confronted him about this?"

"Yes," I said, putting more emotion into the single syllable than I'd intended.

"I take it it didn't go well," Hennix said.

"No. He reacted violently. And he got drunk last night. I should have waited to talk with you."

"Sorry I wasn't available yesterday. Don't beat yourself up over your decision. You're the man on the scene. You've got to do what you think is best."

"Thanks," I said.

"I don't know what to tell you off the top of my head. What you're describing isn't as unusual as you might think. We've spoken with a lady in just the last few weeks with a similar experience. She's a recent widow, married thirty years. She still feels her husband's presence around the house, or calls out to him without thinking, as though he's in the next room. She even sees him sometimes. A hundred years ago, they might have called it a haunting. Now we see it as a mind that's obsessed with images of a lost person. A mind that won't let go.

"Then there's a grieving behavior I call 'somewhere else.' It's the thought that the loved one is nearby, but out of sight. At home while the grieving person is at work, for example, or just in the next room. It takes the unnatural, unmanageable separation of death and reduces it to the normal, bearable kind of separation that we're all used to. A person too in control to pretend to see a loved one might still fall into the habit of thinking that the dead person is about to walk through the front door or is waiting at home."

I thought of the way Harry had smiled as he took his morning walk. "That would fit," I said. Listening to Hennix's slow, rational voice had a calming effect. I understood that it was a professional technique, but I was still comforted by it. "You make it sound like my friend's behavior isn't that abnormal."

"Hey Keane, we both grew up in the sixties. We don't talk *normal* or *abnormal*. Who knows normal? The terms to keep in mind for behavior are *healthy* and *destructive*. In a bereavement, it can be a tough call. What gets one person through could hold another person back. I don't think what your friend is doing is healthy, but it could be a lot worse. In addition to illness, widowed people have a high rate of suicide."

"Yes," I said. "It could be worse."

"There's another angle that's occurred to me. One thing that's guaranteed to complicate a bereavement is guilt. I've read that a person who can't resolve feelings of guilt involving a dead person will keep the dead soul alive mentally as a way of coping."

Guilt again, I thought, remembering Father Peter's hunch. "I've already looked into that," I said. "It didn't pan out."

"Just thought I'd mention it."

"What should I do now?"

"This friend of yours, does he have any family?"

"Yes," I said. "That's how I came to be involved."

"Talk to them. This guy needs their support. He also needs counseling. I'll be happy to recommend somebody. If he wants to call me, I'll talk to him."

"Thanks," I said again, feeling considerably less isolated.

"The bad thing with the sudden loss of a spouse is the unfinished business," Hennix said. "You're an old celibate seminarian, so you don't know, but in a marriage, there are a lot of peaks and valleys, fussing and making up. There are always loose ends to tie up, things to make right. And you do make them right. That's how two people bump along together year after year. But when you're suddenly cut off, maybe with some fixing up left undone, it can go hard. Unfinished business."

I steadied my head against the aluminium phone box. I could have enlightened Hennix, if I'd been in the mood to talk about myself. Not-so-celibate ex-seminarians could get cut off between an injury and an apology, too. I thought of Diana Lord and felt an ache. Then I remembered Mary Ohlman and Father

Peter's inspired guess that I still had unfinished business from that old failure. I was tempted for a moment to discuss my own problems with Hennix. It would have been a comfort to have had his slow, friendly voice explain them all away. But I knew I wouldn't mention either subject, Diana or Mary. It wasn't just that I was calling on Harry's dime. The obstacle was something like professional pride, the odd idea that I'd have to untangle my own mysteries if I was ever to solve anyone else's.

"You there, Keane?"

"I'm here."

"Talk to your friend. Talk to his family. Keep an eye on him. I'll be here if you need me, but you're the man on the case. I meant what I said before. Follow your feelings on this. I wouldn't say that to everybody. You stay on the job."

"I will," I said.

SIXTEEN

I DECIDED TO make good on my promise to Hennix right away, and started off for Harry's cottage. On the way, I stopped by the lake shore where I'd sat earlier watching for the divers. They were gone now, along with the rowboat and the rescue truck. A lone Spring Lake patrol car sat at the curb. It was manned by Archer, the patrolman who had shared my vigil. He smiled as I walked up. On a better day, I might have asked him whether he'd been influenced in his career choice by reading the adventures of Lew Archer, Ross MacDonald's fictional private eye. As it was, I settled for a status report.

"The divers had to rest," Archer said. "Regulations. There's a crew coming in from Point Pleasant to take the next shift. Should be here any minute." He checked to see that we weren't being overheard. "I'd hold the good thought if I were you. The chief stopped by. She said there'd been some developments."

O'Malia hadn't shared any of the details of these developments with Archer, or he'd have known that I was now one of the bad guys. I thanked him and moved on.

I walked around the lake, avoiding the footbridge and its associations. Harry's front door stood open behind the locked screen door. I knocked on the door frame—softly, in deference to the early hour—but there was no answer. Then I circled around to the rear of the house, intending to try the back door. As I turned the final corner, I saw Harry seated on the back steps.

He was dressed as he had been when he'd climbed from the Belmar patrol car, in black sweat pants and a tee shirt. Frank Capoletti's story about finding Harry on the beach was supported by the physical evidence: there was still sand on one leg of his sweats. The bottle of whiskey that had decorated Harry's mantel was now open on the step beside him. He had a small sketch pad on his lap and he was bent over it, working away intently with a pencil.

I was only a few feet from him when he finally looked up. "Damn," he said. "I was just having some hair of the dog that bit me. I didn't expect the actual dog."

"Hello yourself," I said. "I've come to finish our talk."

Harry resumed working on his sketch. "I'm busy," he said.

"It's me or your father, Harry. Take your pick."

Harry grunted. "Bad news, Owen. I told the senior off yesterday. Did such a thorough job of it, in fact, that he ripped the junior off my name, like they rip the buttons off dishonored cavalry officers on television. I'm just plain Harry Ohlman now, with a little torn spot at the end."

Harry must have been drinking since he'd gotten back. He wasn't unsteady, and his speech wasn't slurred, but he was flushed with the strange conceit drinkers sometimes get, the idea that they can understand the world's non sequiturs and see the hidden joints of the universe.

"I probably don't need to be telling you this," Harry continued. "You probably observed the whole ugly episode from your hiding place in the azalea bushes.''

"I saw your father leave," I said.

"Owen Sherlock Keane. Sees all, understands nothing." He looked up from the pad. "That's the Keane curse, by the way. You have to put your finger in the wounds before you believe, and that chance doesn't come along very often. You have to see something to understand it, in a world where you never see the really important things."

"This just occur to you?" I asked.

"Not to me, Owen." He held up the pad. He was working on a portrait of his dead wife. He held it toward me now like a cross held up before a vampire. "That's what herself always said about you. She had you figured out."

Harry's pencil work was more refined than his charcoal sketches. Its sharpness made me realize that in only five months my memory of Mary's face had lost focus, which hurt a little. I kept the emotion out of my voice. "It's a good likeness," I said, nodding toward the sketch.

My compliment didn't please Harry. He looked at the drawing critically. "It's not right yet," he said. "I'm trying for the way she looked on the morning of Amanda's first birthday. Is that overreaching, do you think? It was a perfect late summer morning. Mary wore that day like a designer outfit. An exclusive, made especially for her. I'll get it, eventually. I've got the rest of my life, after all."

"In the meantime," I said, "there's someone I want you to call. His name is Hennix. He wants to talk things over with you. Confidentially."

"A shrink?" Harry asked. He shook his head. "I've tried that. It's just confession with no little room to kneel in and no absolution at the end. Besides, I'm straight now. I'm doing fine."

"You're not getting any better," I said. "You're not getting over it."

"Getting over Mary, you mean? That's something you should know a little about, Owen. Did you ever get over her?" Harry set the sketch down and picked up his bottle. "I expect to do a little better than you in that respect. Of course, I have certain advantages denied you. She was a real woman for me, after all, not some idealized memory getting rosier as the years went by. I saw her first thing in the morning, remember. Every morning. And I can still hear her nagging at me about my smoking and twenty or so other imperfections." He paused as if to listen to her voice. "And, of course, I know the big secret."

"Which is?"

"Mary had a bad back." Harry smiled happily at that empty punch line. "Total blank for you right? Dad really can pick them."

I'd had all I could take of Harry's boozy ramblings. "Mary would be disappointed with you, Harry," I said.

That sobered him slightly. "No 'would be' about it, Owen. We both disappointed her. You were first. You probably think you broke her heart when you ran off to the seminary. You didn't. She was relieved. You gave her an out, which she wanted, and it made her think you might actually end up happy, which she also wanted. That, as we know, didn't happen. Still, she got away from you, which was the important thing."

He took a long drink from the bottle and delivered his next line to the sketch. "Mary wanted a guy who understood those important, invisible things I mentioned earlier. Who could maybe even paint them so that other people could understand them. She got a lawyer instead."

He looked up at me. "Maybe you should use that shrink's number yourself, Owen. You're looking a little green. I'd say you and I are finally even now at the end of a long, long tally. What do you say we call it quits?"

He picked up his pencil and bent down again over his sketch. I turned and left the way I'd come.

SEVENTEEN

PAT O'MALIA'S OFFICE was on the second floor of the Spring Lake municipal building. The building was named for a John J. Rainey, and I wondered as I entered if Rainey was the grandfather O'Malia had told me about, the one who'd been mayor forever. Like most everything in town, the Rainey building was old and solid. The steps I climbed to the second floor were worn stone, and the heavy railing was oak, stained almost black by a long line of sweating palms that ended with my own.

O'Malia's door was open. She was seated at her desk, talking on the phone with her head down. I paused at the threshold and examined the office. The room was smaller than I'd expected, but the ceiling was high and the decorations were first-class. The carpet was a rich, dark green that Harry and Mary's horsey friends the Nickelsons would have admired. The papered walls were dotted with large framed photographs of Spring Lake landmarks. On a mahogany credenza that sat behind O'Malia and her mahogany desk were more photos, these of large, curly-haired dogs. Behind the credenza were tall, small-paned windows through which the sound of the Sunday morning traffic came in to us.

O'Malia hung up the phone and sat looking at it reprovingly, as though it had personally let her down. She had yet to look up at me, and I was about to announce my arrival when she surprised me by saying, "Come in and take a seat."

She left that bit of legerdemain unexplained. Maybe I'd tripped a silent alarm on my way up the stairs, or perhaps it was just that the clock on her credenza was striking ten and she took promptness for granted. I noticed that her suit coat was missing. I restrained the nervous desire to look around for it as I sat down.

O'Malia's irritating cheerfulness was gone, and I missed it. Without the irreverent smile, her heavy features looked menacing. She tapped a yellow legal pad with a gold pen several times like a conductor calling an orchestra to attention. "Let's start at the beginning," she said. "Exactly what is your business in Spring Lake?"

I'd already made up my mind to tell her anything she wanted to know. My interview with Harry had left me too numb to be creative. I began by telling her the bare facts of Mary's death and of Harold Ohlman, Sr.'s, request that I look into the mystery of his son's behavior.

"Why you?" O'Malia asked.

"I worked for the Ohlmans once, years ago."

"As an investigator?"

"As a researcher. I happened to solve a mystery for them." And lost my job over it, I added to myself. "And I was a friend of Harry's."

O'Malia was still sensitive to subtle meanings in verb tenses. "Was his friend?" she asked.

"Am his friend," I said firmly, in an effort to convince us both.

"Go on."

I described my investigation into Harry's bereavement. When I mentioned Father Peter, O'Malia interrupted again. "How is Peter Marruca involved?"

"He's been counseling Harry, at Mr. Ohlman's request."

Up to that point in my story, O'Malia had leaned forward on her elbows, listening intently, but with a puckered expression that I interpreted as official displeasure. Now, as I described the conclusion of my investigation, her tightly drawn lips relaxed, and her narrowed eyes opened wide.

"The poor guy," she said. "So that's why he told Helen Glass his wife was with him."

"She tends to supply a lot of the conversation," I said. "She probably assumed that Mary was with him. Harry just went along with it."

O'Malia dismissed that distinction with a wave of her golden pen. "So if your friend hasn't been drinking, how did he end up drunk on Belmar beach?"

"He wasn't drinking before. I confronted him yesterday evening about the game he's been playing. That set off the drinking." O'Malia's expression was sliding toward puckered again. I helped it along by adding, "He's drinking right now."

Spring Lake's public safety director considered me for some time. Then she tore the blank sheet from the top of her pad and set it aside. "Let's move on for the moment," she said. "Tell me how you came to be involved with Diana Lord."

I described almost meeting Diana at St. Brigid's rectory and her breakfast visit the next morning at the inn. "She wanted my help," I said. "She's in some kind of trouble."

"Some kind of trouble," O'Malia repeated with wistful sarcasm. "Did she ever actually ask for your help?"

"No," I said.

"What did she tell you about this marriage she was running away from?"

"She never mentioned it. Father Peter told me about it." I considered telling O'Malia about the clue I'd found in Diana's bedroom, the card from Paul, but her sour look dissuaded me.

"Do yourself a favor," O'Malia advised. "Don't cite Peter Marruca as your authority. As far as I'm concerned, you two babes wandered out of the same woods." That crack cheered her long enough for a shadow of her earlier smile to appear. "Let's talk about this business of Brigid Kelly. How did Lord find out about her?"

"Father Peter told her, I think. He mentioned the drowning to me in connection with a book he's writing about St. Brigid's. He told me later that Diana must have been asking around town about Brigid, because she'd found out more about her than Peter knows himself."

"That wouldn't require much legwork. Marruca hasn't been here long enough to memorize the zip code."

"Diana thinks that Brigid died for love," I said. "She was impressed by that. It seemed to strike a chord for her. And Peter told me that Diana seemed obsessed with death, and that a lot of the questions she asked had to do with death and the Church's teaching on it."

"And she told you that she swam in the lake every night," O'Malia added. "I can understand why you took that stunt of hers for a suicide. It would all tie together if we had found her in the lake, which we haven't, and if she hadn't cleaned out her house, which she has."

She leaned back in her padded desk chair. "Since I saw you at the Coryell place, I've been trying to get a line on Diana Lord using the Philadelphia address she gave Helen Glass. Its being Sunday hasn't helped, but I'm fairly certain that the name and address she used are both phony."

O'Malia swiveled her chair around until she could look out at her town. "I should have been onto her sooner. I'd heard about her, of course. She's turned a few heads around here over the past month, and not just the male ones. Her regular trips to St. Brigid's rectory have had the tongues of both sexes wagging." She turned her chair back to face me. "Did you know, by the way, that she only used cash?"

I disappointed her by nodding yes.

"That alone should have tipped me. No charge cards or checking account numbers to trace. I don't know how an old sharpie like Helen Glass let herself be taken in. But she was taken in, and so was Father Peter Marruca, the bright hope of the Vatican. It's not the first time he's followed a skirt into trouble, from what I hear. That leaves Mr. Owen Keane and the problem of what to do with him."

She looked me over for a long, uncomfortable minute. "You're my first, by the way," she said.

"Your first what?" I asked.

"Amateur detective. You're the first one I've ever come across in the here and now. You see them all the time on television. Always makes me grind the porcelain off my caps. Some little old lady crime-solver or, pardon me, some asinine gentleman sleuth, the kind of guy who looks like he routinely puts his underwear on backwards but who is, in reality, Albert Einstein. They come in, blunder around, and solve the mystery. I hate that kind of fiction."

I like it myself. It confirms my fondly held belief that we are all amateur detectives, trying to make sense of our own lives, wandering around looking for clues to the basic question: "How the hell did I get here?" I was asking myself that as O'Malia turned the knife.

"Here we have the real-life result of amateur detecting," she said. "Serious screwing up."

O'Malia stood and walked around behind my chair. From the way her voice rose and fell, I deduced that she was pacing back and forth. "Let me summarize," she said. "First we have the case of Harry Ohlman, a widower whose family is afraid he's been drinking to forget. As it turns out, he hasn't been drinking. But now, after only two weeks of your ministrations, he's getting so blind he can't find his way home at night.

"Since you had your evenings free, you took on yet another mystery, this one involving a beautiful stranger with an unmentionable problem. Turns out she's a con artist, a virtuoso on the naive upright, and she plays you like a Steinway. This is in her spare time, when she's not tickling the ivories over at the rectory. She feeds you all the right lines, and pretty soon you feel like you've landed in a Bogart movie and Bacall is offering you whistling lessons."

"Why?" I asked the empty desk chair. "Why would she bother? What was she supposed to be after?"

O'Malia's answer came from somewhere to my left. "I'd say laughs, if I were guessing. Money maybe. Maybe she thought you had some. You've been giv-

ing a fair imitation of it. Then again, it might just have
been for kicks. Maybe she was living out a fantasy, like
your old friend Harry. Maybe while you were tearing
one dream world down you were helping to build another one up. Nice irony there.

"Whatever Diana Lord's motivation was, Harry
Ohlman was damn lucky she happened along. If you'd
been able to concentrate your peculiar gifts entirely on
his problem, he'd be looking at liver damage by now."

I'd been put down often enough to qualify as an
expert recipient, and I was impressed by O'Malia's
technique. She knew just where to hit and how hard to
do it. Ordinarily, this kind of emotional working over
would have had me reeling like a paperback detective
who'd been beaten up by the assistant heavies. Not this
time though. This time I had a secret remedy, an article of faith that sustained me. O'Malia was wrong
about Diana Lord. I didn't know what Diana's problem was, but I'd seen it in her eyes and I knew it was
real. It was no con and it was no joke. If O'Malia
could be wrong about that, she could be wrong about
other things. Maybe even about Mr. Owen Keane.

O'Malia reappeared in my field of vision and sat
down again at her desk. "So what do you intend to do
about this nutty friend of yours?"

"He isn't nuts," I said with deliberate slowness. I
was more offended by that idea than I had been by her
long, unflattering assessment of my work. "He's
hurting."

She held up one hand like a traffic cop signaling a
stop. "Sorry. That was a stupid thing to say. But I have
a responsibility to this town. If Harry Ohlman is a
danger to anybody, including himself, it's my business."

"Harry isn't going to bother anyone. Until I showed up, nobody even knew he was here."

O'Malia reacted to my show of anger by getting mad herself. "Don't remind me of that if you expect me to trust your judgment," she said. "Your friend needs help. Professional help."

"I know he does," I said, really admitting it to myself for the first time as I spoke the words aloud.

I stood up. My exchange with O'Malia had shocked me out of the fog I'd been in since I'd left Harry. I'd come to a decision, or rather a decision had come to me. "You'll be happy to know I'm taking myself off Harry's case. That's the way he wants it, and he needs to have things his way. I'll turn over what I've found to his family. Then it'll be their call."

"I think that's best," O'Malia said. She stood up and followed me as far as the door of her office. "Check in with me before you leave Spring Lake. I might be able to give you some news. I still intend to find out the truth about this Diana Lord."

You and me both, I thought.

EIGHTEEN

I'D STARTED THE DAY mad at myself for being a step behind everyone else in Spring Lake. Now I found that I was even falling behind Owen Keane. Only an hour earlier, I had promised Edward Hennix that I would stand by Harry. Now, with no real forethought, I'd told Pat O'Malia that I was getting out. My latest decision had come from the heart, meaning that it was an emotional reaction to Harry's anger and O'Malia's criticism. Given time, the rationalization department in my head would come up with some nobler reasons for it. For the moment, I was driven only by the urge to get it over with.

I couldn't wait the five minutes it would take me to walk back to the Gascony. I hurried instead to the drugstore that shared an intersection with the John J. Rainey building. I made my way across the crowded front of the store, sidestepping weekend visitors and squeezing between a cardboard display case of suntan lotion and a pyramid of bright plastic sand buckets. My goal was an old wooden phone booth in the corner. Mr. Ohlman had neglected to tell me where he was staying in New York City. So I dialed the number of Masthead Farm, the Ohlman's Cape Cod retreat.

A man answered the phone. After I had identified myself, the man said, "This is Ralph. Mr. and Mrs. Ohlman took the baby away for the weekend. They can't be reached."

I pictured the handyman seated in Mr. Ohlman's easy chair, drinking a cold beer and watching a baseball game. "This is important," I said.

"Doesn't matter," Ralph replied before hanging up.

I sat with my eyes closed holding the droning receiver to my ear. "I'm so bad at this job I can't even resign," I said aloud. Then I remembered Father Peter Marruca. He'd been watching over Harry before I'd taken the case. He could cover for me until the Ohlmans came up with a new plan.

I left the store and hurried off to St. Brigid's. On my way around the lake, I passed Harry's cottage, but pointedly ignored it. My goal was the old brick rectory. While I was still half a block away, the front door of the church opened. Helen Glass came out, followed by Father Peter. He was wearing full vestments, topped by a green silk chasuble that shone in the bright sunlight. I stopped in my tracks and watched as the pair slowly descended the front steps, Mrs. Glass speaking rapidly and Father Peter listening with his head bowed. He stopped on the final step, and she said her good-byes looking back up at him. Then she climbed into a white Cadillac that was parked at the curb. I looked around for a place to hide in case she came my way, but she drove off to the south instead.

I hurried on, anxious to catch the priest before he got away. I needn't have worried. Peter stood frozen on the step, watching the place where the white car had been parked.

"Hello," I called while I was still some distance from him.

The priest's head snapped around like a disturbed sleeper's. His startled expression quickly hardened into a grimace, the transformation reminding me that we hadn't parted on good terms. His opening remark picked up one of the themes he'd explored on the day I'd chauffeured him around. "You wouldn't listen," he said. "I told you she was out of your league." He spoke quietly, without his previous rancor, his light, high voice almost wavering. He looked out at the calm blue water before him. "Now see what you've done."

Across the lake another rescue truck had parked behind the Spring Lake patrol car. It belonged to the Point Pleasant crew Archer had promised me.

"Diana isn't in the lake, if that's what you're thinking," I said.

Peter told me that was old news by shrugging. "What do you want now?" he asked.

"Two things. I want you to look after Harry until his family replaces me. I'm resigning."

Peter took the blow well. His obvious indifference settled a debate I was having with myself. I wouldn't share Harry's secret with him.

"What's the other request?" he asked.

"I'm going to find Diana Lord. I want your help. I want you to tell me everything you know about her."

Peter turned to examine me. He was still standing on the step, which put our eyes on the same level. "Why would I tell you anything?" he asked.

"Think of it as practice," I said. "Pat O'Malia's going to be asking for the same information before the day is over."

"That one," Peter said resignedly. "She doesn't like me very much. Father Palladay, my predecessor, baptized her. He was part of the old crowd that ran this town. She can't stand to see an outsider in his place."

"She doesn't approve of us in general," I said, trying to reestablish some link between the priest and myself. "Let's talk about Diana. Did she mention anything about her family or where they live?"

Peter had resumed his examination of the lake. "Only that they have money. The marriage she'd run out on was almost an arranged one. At least it seemed intended to please her parents."

"Her fiancé was rich?"

"Yes, but he was a self-made man. Worked his way up from nothing. Diana seemed proud of that, but it didn't keep her from running out on the guy."

"What was the fiancé's name?"

"She didn't say. I don't know his name or his business or anything else about him."

"Did she ever mention the name Paul?"

"No. I'm not being difficult, Owen. I'm not sure I'd tell you if I did know something definite about Diana. As it happens, I don't have to make that judgment. She was careful not to give me specific information. I can see that now. She told me just enough to accomplish her purpose, whatever that was."

Like O'Malia, the priest had come to see the Diana we had known as a disguise. "What do you think her purpose was?" I asked.

Peter smiled unexpectedly and without humor. "To test me," he said. "That's a silly, egotistical thought, isn't it? But that's what I was thinking before you walked up. She was a test for me.

"I don't know why on earth I would tell you that. Do people tend to blurt things out to you?"

"I've been told that I inspire rambling." And that I was obsessed with forgiving sins, I added to myself.

Harry had made that last observation a long time ago. It seemed relevant to me suddenly, as I remembered O'Malia's passing remark about some other woman trouble in the priest's past.

"You told me that you were exiled to Spring Lake because of your political writing. That wasn't the real reason."

"No," Peter said. "That was a lie. And I didn't need your help the other day because my car is in the shop. I don't even have a car. My license has been suspended.

"This has all happened to me before. There was another young woman, I mean. A year or so ago. Before I came here. I wrecked a car one night while I was driving her home from a wedding reception. She wasn't hurt badly, thank God. I wasn't either." He rubbed the scar on his forehead. "Except for my reputation.

"That's why I thought of Diana as a test. I should have locked her out of the rectory, but I wouldn't take the easy way out. I wanted to prove something through her. To myself, I guess. That the first episode had really been innocent. Instead, I ended up in another wreck. With lipstick on my collar," he added with a rueful smile. "This time, instead of a tree, I ran into a failed priest. Someone who didn't measure up to my standards, someone I looked down on, frankly. That makes my comeuppance complete.

"It's all so tied together somehow." He held his hands out before him and wove invisible patterns in the air with his nervous fingers. "Everything echoing something else, patterns being repeated. It has to mean something."

" 'It must tend to some end, or else our universe is ruled by chance, which is unthinkable.' "

"Who are you quoting?" Peter asked. "Chesterton?"

"Sherlock Holmes," I said. Peter's mention of patterns repeating themselves reminded me of another area I wanted to explore. "Tell me about Brigid Kelly."

"Why?"

"Brigid's story meant something to Diana, the same way Diana showing up on your doorstep echoed a past event for you. If I can understand Brigid's history, it could give me some insight into Diana."

Peter shook his head at that. "I don't know enough to help you, I'm afraid. Brigid was roughly Diana's age when she died. She drowned in the lake. At the time, Spring Lake was more than the ornamental pond it is now. There was boating and swimming. I haven't really done much digging yet on Brigid's drowning. Diana seemed convinced that it was related to a love affair."

"I know," I said.

"Don't ask me where she got that idea. It wasn't from me. Come into the church for a moment. There's something you might as well see." I followed him up the steps, looking down at my tiny midday shadow as it followed the right angles of hot stone.

"As I think I told you before," Peter said, "Brigid's father, Thomas Kelly, commissioned the church in her memory. He was some kind of railroad tycoon. At the turn of the century, Spring Lake was a watering place for the Irish nouveau riche."

He held a tall bronze door open for me, and I stepped into the cool semidarkness of a broad foyer.

"The church has air conditioning, but we almost never turn it on. The thickness of the stone seems to keep the place as cool as an icehouse." He led me across the foyer. We walked silently on floors that appeared to be made of varnished cork. The wooden door of the nave stood open. The space beyond the door was smaller than I'd expected. That was my initial impression, at least. Once we'd stepped inside, I was struck by the height of the ceiling and the volume of damp air above me. Staring up into the darkened dome made me feel dizzy.

I dropped my gaze and examined the main altar. Its gold decorations seemed to catch and hold the faint light coming in through the rich rose and blue windows. There were tall paintings on either side of the altar. They appeared flat and lifeless in the dull light, as though covered with dust. The only color that stood out from them was the sky blue of the Virgin's dress.

Peter gave me a moment to take in the church. Then he led me toward a deep alcove off to our right. I thought at first that it was a side altar, but it only held a tall rack of pamphlets and tracts. The alcove was lit by a single stained-glass window that depicted a saint in browns and golds against a field of emerald green. St. Brigid, the Gothic lettering of a banner at her feet told me.

"St. Brigid is the patroness of Ireland, of course," the priest said, "but I'm told that this window is actually a likeness of Brigid Kelly." The face was square and solid and as white as chalk, with large brown eyes that stared down at us from under black brows.

"She's here in the floor," Father Peter said.

"What?" I asked, confused.

He knelt on the floor near a patch of gold cast down
by the window and brushed his fingers over words cut
into the stone. "Brigid Deirdre Kelly," he read. "Born
1891, died 1910."

Father Peter had shown no imagination when he'd
compared the moist coolness of his church to an icehouse. The coolness of the black, weedy bottom of the
lake would have been a better image. Or the damp cold
of a crypt.

NINETEEN

MY FEET were dragging as I left Father Peter, and my day had just begun. I barely paid attention to the path I was following around the southern end of the lake. Something the priest had said was spreading through my tired brain like a shot of liquor. It was the idea that everything in Spring Lake echoed something else. I felt the same dumb wonder I'd heard in Peter's quiet voice. It was certainly odd that Peter's and Harry's pasts should share such an obvious parallel: automobile accidents had scarred them both and had changed the straight and narrow course of their lives. It was just as odd that Peter and I should be thrown together, failing priest and failed priest. Peter was a stranger to us, but our three lives seemed to have tangles that went back years. It was as though the small-town atmosphere of Spring Lake, where everyone was related somehow and knew one another's secrets, had affected us, jumbling our pasts like pieces of different jigsaw puzzles shaken up inside a small box.

The town had worked the same spell on Diana Lord, another transient, now hopelessly mixed up with the priest's unquiet past and with the story of a girl who had drowned in the lake. Diana was fascinated by a memory and by the idea of becoming a memory. She was already an echo of the past for Father Peter and for me, an echo of my old failure with Mary. The connection there was the feeling of being cut off prematurely—the feeling of what Edward Hennix had called "unfinished business."

After stopping at Archer's patrol car long enough to confirm that nothing had been found by the Point Pleasant divers, I returned to the Gascony. I was looking for my landlord, George Metelis. After several inquiries, I found him in a second-floor bathroom. He was standing with a rubber plug in one hand and a can of drain cleaner in the other, staring forlornly at a tub of soapy water.

"Hello," I said from the open doorway.

Metelis returned my greeting with an oddly guilty smile. It occurred to me that I'd caught him in an activity he considered beneath his dignity. "Drain's clogged," he said.

We watched the gray water not drain for a moment. Then I said: "I need some information. Local information."

Metelis brightened noticeably. "What's up?" he asked.

"I'm trying to find out all I can about a girl named Brigid Kelly. She drowned in Spring Lake in 1910."

Metelis began to twirl the plug he held by its beaded metal chain. "That's ancient history," he said. "You want one of the old-timers. We call them the founding families. 'We' being the new arrivals, the people who are making something of this town. They aren't too fond of us. 'They' being the people who were letting the place rot. There's a lady who's supposed to be a local historian. Not as uppity as some of them. Nice actually. Try her."

He looked back down at the tub, so I did, too. The water looked like it would dry up before it would drain. "What's her name?" I asked.

"Mrs. Dial. Claire Dial. Runs an Irish import shop over on the main drag. The Cashel House."

The image of jumbled puzzles came to mind again. I'd already met Claire Dial in connection with Harry's mystery. Now it could be that she held a clue to Diana's.

I thanked Metelis and started off for the Cashel House. I made the short trip into town by car to save my tired legs. Spring Lake's single street of shops was already crowded with Sunday visitors and parking spaces were at a premium. So was floor space in the Cashel House, where browsers blocked most of the narrow aisles. With many false starts and turnings, I made my way to the sales counter. Behind it, a young woman was ringing up purchases. She was college age, Diana's age, but the easy smile and happy expression made her seem like Diana's antithesis. When I asked for Claire Dial, she directed me toward the open office door at the back of the shop. I worked my way slowly back through the maze, wondering as I went whether Mrs. Dial had gotten the morning news bulletin from Helen Glass. If she had, I might be as welcome in her shop as a Union Jack.

Claire Dial was running figures through a desktop calculator with a practiced hand. I waited until she had totaled before knocking on the door frame.

"Hello," she said. "Did you catch up with Mr. Ohlman?"

Her friendly smile let me relax a little. "Yes and no," I replied. "Can I bother you for a moment? I've been told that you're an authority on local history."

The old woman smiled at that. Her desk sat beneath a skylight, and the sun made her gray hair seem almost silver. Her eyes were still young, though. They reminded me of the happy, open eyes of the girl behind the counter. "Come in," Mrs. Dial said. "What can I help you with?"

I repeated the request that I'd already made to Father Peter and George Metelis.

"Poor Brigid's very popular all of a sudden," Mrs. Dial said. "There was someone in here asking about her just the other day. Father Peter's young friend," she added with a small movement of her shoulders that might have been a shudder.

She meant Diana Lord, of course. I noted the implied criticism of Peter Marruca, but I was more interested in Mrs. Dial's confirmation that I was on the right track. "Did she say why she was interested in Brigid's story?" I asked.

"No," Mrs. Dial replied. "But I've never had a more attentive audience. Why is Brigid of interest to you, young man?"

"I saw her grave this morning in the church. I'm curious about how she came to be there. No one seems to know much about it. I asked George Metelis, my landlord at the Gascony. He recommended you."

Mrs. Dial returned Metelis's good opinion of her. "A nice man," she said. "He and his wife went to a lot of trouble to duplicate the original colors of their guesthouse. They've done a very nice job, don't you think? They asked my advice on some decorating points, like the wicker in the breakfast room. That's just as it was a hundred years ago."

"The past repeating itself," I said, almost to myself.

"Yes," Mrs. Dial agreed happily. "Of course, Mr. Metelis is a newcomer, so he doesn't know the local history. The old stories and the old scandals. Brigid figured in one of the scandals, I'm afraid.

"Her father, Thomas Kelly, was the president of the East Jersey Line. A railroad, you know. There was a lot of railroad money in Spring Lake at the turn of the century. The Kellys lived in a big house on the lake. It burned down sometime during the Depression. The family didn't rebuild it. They couldn't afford to build mansions by then.

"When she was eighteen, Brigid fell in love with a young man who worked for her father. An ivy-leaguer named Cyrus Oberting. My mother said she could remember them out rowing together on the lake, Cy Oberting in a striped jacket and straw hat and Brigid under a parasol. Everyone thought that he wanted to marry the boss's daughter and expected that he would. But he didn't. One fine day, Oberting moved out to California, lock, stock, and barrel. The accident occurred about a week later. Brigid's drowning, I mean. She was found in the lake wearing a fancy gown, the one she'd worn to the Fourth of July ball, when she'd waltzed the night through with Cy Oberting."

Mrs. Dial's pink face settled into a sweet smile as she stared over my shoulder at the twirling dancers. A fragment of my wasted education came to mind: the image of the doomed Ophelia from *Hamlet,* pulled down into the water by her clothes "heavy with their drink."

"How exactly did Brigid come to drown?" I asked.

"No one knows exactly." Mrs. Dial emphasized the last word in a gentle reproof. "Brigid went to bed that last night as usual. Cried herself to sleep over Cy Oberting, or so her family thought. The next morning, an empty rowboat was seen in the center of the lake. Poor Brigid was found sometime afterward.

"She died of a broken heart, you see, and no woman had more cause."

I waited for her to explain that, and after a discreet pause, she did. "Brigid was in the family way, as we used to say. It wasn't just Brigid whom Oberting deserted. It was also the fruit of their love. Brigid couldn't stand that denial. It was like being torn in two. Cy Oberting killed her as surely as if he had shot her through the heart."

It was impossible not to picture the Oberting of the story twirling his black moustache like the villain of a melodrama. For that's what the story was in the end, a Victorian melodrama, sans hero. That quality explained its attraction to Claire Dial, the local historian. It was a period piece as perfect for its setting as the wicker furniture she had recommended for the Gascony. The story was too perfect, in fact. It needed corroborating.

"Are there any Kellys still living around here?" I asked.

"Oh no. Not since the big house burned down in the thirties. The family had fallen on hard times by then, because of the crash, of course, and because of St. Brigid's."

"I understand that Thomas Kelly built the church."

"Yes," Mrs. Dial said, suddenly solemn. "Spent most of his fortune on it, poor man."

The "poor man" suggested another story, or at least a second act to Brigid's melodrama. "Tell me about that," I said.

Mrs. Dial looked toward the open office door and lowered her already soft voice. "I shouldn't really. It was just old loose talk. No one really knew how Brigid came to drown, you see. It could have been an accident, after all. Could very well have been."

She paused expectantly, and I nodded in agreement. Having made that concession to the lofty view, Mrs. Dial moved on. "The loose talk held that her death was a suicide and that Brigid had no right to be buried by the Church, never mind in a church. Those tongues said that Thomas Kelly had struck a deal with the bishop. St. Brigid's was the price he paid for his daughter's funeral service. He bought her way into heaven."

He'd gotten off cheaply enough for that, I thought.

"The shadow of that scandal has never been off the poor church," Mrs. Dial said. "It's always been a cold, formal place, despite the fine work of Father Palladay and his predecessors."

She and her church were about to weather another scandal, though she didn't appear to know it yet. I wondered if Mrs. Dial would connect Diana's disappearance with the "shadow" that had darkened the old church and be secretly satisfied by the echo of Brigid's story.

I'd begun to rise from my chair when Mrs. Dial had another thought. "There is Sister Theresa Kelly, of course. She would have been Brigid's cousin. She lived here in Spring Lake as a girl, I know, because she and my mother were great friends. We still exchange notes at Christmas time, Sister Theresa and I. The dear soul is almost ninety." Mrs. Dial glanced at the card file on her desk top but didn't consult it. "She lives in her order's retirement home in Ocean City. St. Cynthia's Home. As far as I know, she's the last of the family."

An old black phone on the desk rang out shrilly. "Excuse me," Mrs. Dial said to me before addressing the handset. "Cashel House. Helen? Where on earth have you been all morning?"

I was already out of my seat by then, heading for the exit.

Mrs. Dial held her hand over the receiver. "Goodbye, Mr...?"

"Smith," I said from the doorway.

TWENTY

AFTER CLAIRE DIAL'S bedtime story, I should have gone back to my room and turned in. I was tired enough to sleep, even though the sun was high overhead, its heat making Main Street shimmer like a mirage. I was tired, but I couldn't waste time sleeping. Somewhere, Diana Lord was facing her troubles alone. Or not facing them, a possibility I found more frightening. Helping Diana had become my one goal. At least it felt that simple. Had I been rested and alert, I would have realized that my failure with Harry was driving me, too, or rather the shame of it was. I didn't want to fail again with Diana. I was afraid I might be her only hope. It may have been that she was also mine.

By the time I'd walked the half-block to the space where I'd left my rented Chevy, my mind was made up. I'd follow the thread of Brigid Kelly's story for as long as I could hold it. That thread now led me toward Ocean City and a nun who was almost ninety. It was just my kind of clue: fanciful and unlikely. I drove west until I found the Garden State Parkway. Then I headed south.

Every mile I traveled away from Spring Lake made me feel better. Following Father Peter's lead, I'd begun to think that the town was covered by a hopeless tangle of memories and associations like a fairy-tale castle surrounded by a forest of thorns. I wondered now if Harry had sensed that quality, too. He'd cer-

tainly chosen the perfect spot for losing himself in the
dead past. I decided that if I did nothing else for my
onetime friend, I would convince his family to get him
clear of that place.

I had a vague idea that Ocean City was somewhere
near Atlantic City. My uncertainty and the casualness
of my approach to Sister Theresa began to worry me
after I'd driven for an hour or so. I pulled into a service plaza that sat in the center of the divided highway and spent a dollar on a road map. I used an
outside pay phone to call Information and then St.
Cynthia's home. I asked the woman who answered for
Theresa Kelly.

"Sister Theresa never comes to the phone," the
woman told me. "She doesn't get around too well."

"Would she be up to a visit?" I asked.

"Oh, I'm sure she'd be delighted."

I was nowhere near that certain myself, but I pressed
on. The highway was wooded and peaceful now, except for the tour buses carrying the faithful to the Atlantic City casinos. I crossed two good-size rivers, first
the Mullica, on a low bridge from which I caught a
glimpse of white wading birds and open fishing boats,
and then Great Egg Harbor River. It might have been
Great Egg Harbor itself that I crossed and not the river
that fed it. The bridge was certainly long enough and
as high as a five-dollar plane ride. From the crest of
the bridge, I saw a huge power plant, its single
smokestack disguised as a giant lighthouse. Following the directions I'd been given over the phone, I left
the Parkway at the next exit and drove east.

Like many shore communities on the southern Jersey coast, Ocean City was built on a narrow barrier
island. To reach it, I drove across another bridge, a

modest one above a reed-choked bay that smelled like a backed-up drain. Ocean City was unpretentious and made up mostly of rental houses set on streets that paralleled the beach on one side of the island and the marshy bay on the other. The houses on the beach side were large, and they effectively blocked the ocean view. The bay-side homes were modest in comparison. St. Cynthia's was on the bay, an old frame house with gray shingle siding and peeling white trim. The house was identified by a black-and-gold sign on its burnt-out front lawn and by a cross that rose from the peak of the roof.

I was picturing the nuns of my youth as I climbed the front steps of the house, veiled women in ankle-length black habits. The woman who answered the door and pumped my hand wore a sky-blue house dress and canvas boat shoes, and her gray head was bare. She identified herself as Sister Ann Glembocki, director of the home. When she spoke, I recognized her as the woman I had talked with on the phone.

"We were just trying to remember the last visitor Sister Theresa had, and none of us could," Sister Ann said. "It must have been five years ago at least. Sister Theresa has outlived so many of her pupils and all of her family. She's been here in the home for twenty-two years, longer than any of our other residents. Longer than the current staff, too, of course. During the last hurricane scare, it was all we could do to get her evacuated to the mainland. She wanted to go down with the house."

I smiled politely at that, and she got down to business. "May I ask why you're calling today?"

I'd had the last hour to prepare my answer. "I'm researching the history of a town called Spring Lake.

It's on the coast about two hours north of here. Sister Theresa's family were prominent residents of the town around the turn of the century. She lived there herself, I believe, as a girl."

"I didn't know that," Sister Ann said. "How interesting. I'm sure she'll be happy to help you. She's in the day room, waiting for you."

She escorted me down a center hallway that led to the back of the house and a large screened porch. The porch was set up as an activity room, with two card tables in the center and well-padded redwood furniture around the screened walls. In one corner, a portable television was proclaiming the advantages of truck driver training. An old woman in a wheelchair slept in front of the set. Like my guide, the woman wore a blue dress, and, despite the heat, there was a dark blue cardigan draped around her shoulders like a shawl. Her white curly hair was short and thin on top and she wore thick glasses shaped in a dated harlequin-style like the sunglasses of a movie queen from the fifties.

The woman's white head came up slowly when Sister Ann touched her shoulder, and her milky blue eyes examined me carefully while the director introduced me and explained my business.

Once we were alone, Sister Theresa nodded toward the television. "Turn that off, please," she said, "and sit down."

I switched off the television and pulled up a card table chair. Sister Theresa accompanied my activity with a monologue delivered in a rapid, clipped voice.

"They turn that television on to keep me awake, but I make a point of falling asleep right away. It's a defense mechanism against one of the true dangers of the age.''

"What danger?" I asked innocently as I sat down.

"Television, of course," she said. Her head sagged a little to one side and her arms and legs remained immobile, but her rapid speech actually gained speed. "It's the biggest thing since the bomb, bigger maybe, and it just happened. Nobody voted for it, nobody collected signatures. One day nothing and the next day—pow—every home in America. Did you ever think about that? I mean, they can't sell a pill for gas before it passes ninety-two inspections at the FDA. If they put cherry flavoring in it, laboratories from here to the Pacific start feeding it to rats day and night to prove it'll cause cancer. But they can sell you a box to put in your living room that will absolutely change the course of human history and nobody in the government or the laboratories even notices. If you die from the neck up, it's not their business. If you could swallow the blessed things, then they'd notice. It's a shame they don't run on saccharin or nicotine—televisions, I mean. That would get somebody's attention.''

I nodded in agreement and opened my mouth to speak. Sister Theresa never broke stride.

"But no," she said, "they run on electricity and sell a lot of soap and beer and automobiles, so nobody bothers about them. But they, or it, I mean—television—has changed the world. Absolutely changed it. You see it most in the kids. Name one subject that a nine-year-old of 1910 knew more about than his parents. You can't. There wasn't one. But ask the same thing of a nine-year-old today and the answer's obvious. Television. The kids watch hours and hours of it. They know more about the latest fads than their par-

ents possibly could. That's what television really sells:
fads, crazes, new styles. It's the chrome on the Buick,
if you know what I mean. They can't come out with a
new Buick every year, so they change the chrome.
That's all television teaches kids, the latest chrome. No
ideas, no substance. But it's enough to convince the
kids they're smarter than their folks, and they know
more about what's going on. That's the root of ninety
percent of the problems these days. Parents can't pass
on the important things they've learned because the
kids think they know it all. But all they know is the
chrome. They're specialists in chrome."

I thought again of the black-veiled nuns of gram-
mar school. Even without her costume, Sister Theresa was recreating the era for me. She only had to run
me through the multiplication tables to make the ef-
fect complete.

"What did you want to know about Spring Lake?"
she asked.

The abrupt transition caught me unprepared. "I
understand you grew up there," I said.

"I was born there," Sister Theresa corrected. "May
18, 1901. I remember it as a lovely place, which shows
what a little distance in time will do for your point of
view. When I lived there, I thought the town was
stuffy and stilted and hidebound by conventions and
hypocritical morality. Looking back across the troubles of this century makes me more appreciative of
those old conventions and hypocrisies, let me tell
you."

I'd considered using a roundabout route to Brigid
Kelly, but listening to Sister Theresa's rapid-fire delivery made me despair of sneaking up on her. I fell back
on a direct approach. "I understand that you're re-

lated to Brigid Kelly, the girl who drowned in Spring Lake."

"Yes," Sister Theresa said. "She was my cousin." Her hazy blue eyes narrowed behind the movie-star glasses.

"I'd like to know the circumstances of her drowning."

The nun shook her head. "That isn't a fit subject for an article or a history or whatever it is you're working on. Let the poor soul rest in peace."

"I'm not writing an article," I said. "I'm trying to trace a young woman who has disappeared. She's in some kind of trouble, serious trouble. This girl—Diana—was fascinated by Brigid's story, by the idea that Brigid died for love. Diana seemed to identify with it. I'm hoping that if I can understand what happened to Brigid, it will tell me something about Diana and maybe even help me to stop her from following Brigid's example." I surprised myself with that speech. I seemed to listen to it more than deliver it, like a sympathetic third party concerned by the strain and fatigue I heard in my own voice.

Sister Theresa moved her mouth in a chewing motion for a moment. "This Diana has been listening to a lot of nonsense about Brigid," she finally said. "Brigid didn't die for love. She died of despair, God rest her."

"What about Cy Oberting?" I asked.

"That mannequin!" Sister Theresa fired back with a dismissive shake of her white head. "You would as likely die over losing a new hat. I suppose you heard that she was found in a ball gown? Malicious, romantic nonsense. She was wearing a plain cotton dress, but that wasn't dramatic enough for the gossips."

"What did Brigid despair of?" I asked.

"Forgiveness. Her father's forgiveness. Brigid was a sweet girl and a lively one. Maybe a little flighty, as we used to say, but I've seen many a worse one since. I loved her dearly. Her father, my Uncle Thomas, was old to have a daughter her age. He was a formal man and a little austere, but I loved him, too. He was freer with me than he was with Brigid, less strict. Of course I was just a little girl back then. He held the reins on Brigid tightly, too tightly, and showed her too little of his real affection. It made her an easy mark for Cyrus Oberting.

"She ran afoul of him that last summer. He was an empty-headed clothes horse, sick with a love of himself that he carried around like a contagious disease. Brigid caught it from him, and worse, poor girl."

Sister Theresa hesitated at the next jump. I helped her across it. "Brigid became pregnant," I said.

"Yes. Oberting showed his true colors then, when it was too late. Brigid was left with the reality of how foolishly she had misspent herself. In that awful state of mind, she decided that her father would never forgive her, that her sin had cut her off from him. It was that loss that drove her to despair.

"The awful irony is that Thomas Kelly would have forgiven her if she'd given him the chance. As young as I was, I recognized that fact of his suffering. He would have given anything to have forgiven his daughter. His inability to deliver that forgiveness to her broke him. More than his loss, that was what blighted his life.

"He built St. Brigid's Church as almost his last act, in a hopeless attempt to pass that forgiveness on. Oh, the gossips knew better. They claimed the church was a payment in some dirty deal to get Brigid a Christian burial. More malicious nonsense. No one knew enough about her death to rule it anything but an accident. St. Brigid's was no payment. It was the physical manifestation of Uncle Thomas's frustrated forgiveness.''

She sat for a while with her eyes almost closed. When she spoke again, it was at half her previous speed. ''My mind often turned to that church over the years. I began to think of it as a storehouse of hopeless forgiveness, put there by one desperate father, but available to anyone who came looking for it. After a time, it occurred to me that that might be the function of every church everywhere. Of every temple and mosque. That they all might be clearinghouses, places where we go to deposit the forgiveness we can't deliver and where we find the forgiveness that is missing in our lives because we're cut off from our loved ones by the grave. Generation to generation, that forgiveness is built up and distributed over and over, loved one to loved one, stranger to stranger. Does that make any sense?''

''Yes,'' I said.

''It's too terrible otherwise to think of us poor sinners cut off from one another in the darkness, unable to forgive or to be forgiven. Too terrible.''

She roused herself by shaking her head. ''Sometimes I think too much,'' she said in her earlier, rapid style. ''What is the cure for that, I wonder?''

''Television,'' I said as I stood up.

She smiled for the first time. ''Serves me right for going on so about it,'' she said. ''Sorry about the lecture. Habit of a lifetime. Television hasn't really ruined people, you know. I don't mean to sound as though I think it has. It's just isolated us all so. Amazing, isn't it? A magic box that brings the world into your living room and it actually makes you lonely. Thank you for sharing your day with me.''

TWENTY-ONE

As I RECROSSED the Mullica River on my drive north, I noted again the brilliant white birds feeding on the river's grassy shallows. These slender birds seemed important for some reason, and I slowed the Chevy down while my tired mind worked it out. It was the mysterious poem, I finally realized. The wading birds had reminded me of the almost poem that taunted Mrs. Ohlman, the poem about a bird and the ocean. She'd transmitted its echo to me like some slow-acting virus. Now I felt that I could almost remember the poem myself, like some fragment of music from years ago. While I strained to hear it, my guilty conscience had its way with my sleepy powers of reason. How could I say that I'd done everything I could for Harry, it asked me, when I hadn't found that poem?

I hadn't even looked for the poem very thoroughly. I'd asked one or two people about it, but I'd never come up with a better approach. In the old days, when I worked in New York City and did much of my investigating within the four walls of the New York Public Library, I would have put the question of the poem to a certain research assistant named Marilyn Tucci. Marilyn would have found the work, a critical analysis of it, and a biography of the poet, all before lunch. We'd had a relationship that had reached out beyond the library, and I would have valued her opinion now on questions deeper than the name of a poem. Marilyn no longer worked as a research assistant, but that wasn't the real objection to my calling her. She and I were cut off from one other by obstacles that included the holy bonds of matrimony. The other things that stood between us were harder to name but just as serious. We didn't share a view of the world, and Marilyn had made it clear that she would not forsake her facts and figures for my vague mysteries.

The pine forest through which I drove reminded me of the case that had broken my relationship with Marilyn, an investigation into a plane crash in these very woods. That memory led in turn to the name of another person I could ask about the poem: James Skiles, Storyteller of the Pines. I pulled over onto the shoulder and checked my map. There was an exit coming up for Highway 539, which would carry me back into Skiles's realm. That would still leave the considerable challenge of finding the shack he called home, but I decided to try.

I'd met Skiles during my investigation of the plane crash, but we hadn't hit it off. That was due in part to my discovering that he was a fraud. Skiles pretended to be an illiterate storyteller passing on an oral tradition about the Pine Barrens, a huge, sparsely populated area of southeastern New Jersey. He was in fact an educated Philadelphian who had hidden himself away in the forest to escape an unhappy past. Our first meeting had not been a success, but I'd later solved a mystery for him, untangling a bit of the Philadelphia history that had still bound him, and we had become friends.

My concern about finding Skiles's sand road proved to be justified. I drove past it on my first attempt, ending up in Smithtown, a one-horse operation whose horse had died of old age. I turned back south and tried again. This time I spotted an unmarked road at about the right location. I followed it back into the forest, and it led me by slow turnings to Skiles's house.

The single-story frame house had been undergoing repairs when I'd first seen it five years before, and they were still in progress, tar paper substituting for the wooden shingles on one wall and wooden shingles standing in for panes of glass in one of the windows that flanked the peeling, red front door. I left my car in the road and crossed Skiles's sandy front yard, pausing to run my fingers over the handle of a cast-iron water pump that was right where I'd left it. I looked for the old refrigerator that used to sit beside the pump, but it was gone, its place taken by the bare wooden skeleton of a sofa. The latest trend in Pine Barren lawn ornaments, I decided.

Skiles appeared at his door unsummoned, just as he had five years before. He was noticeably older—well past seventy now, to my certain knowledge—his shaggy hair and stubble beard were both pure white. He was also thinner, his loose trousers floating around his waist at the ends of bright red suspenders.

The squinty smile he gave me was the same, though, and the cackling laugh that accompanied his greeting. "Owen Keane," he said. "The stormy petrel of spiritual disorder. How goes the quest? Don't tell me you tracked God to this lonely corner of the map."

"He's tracking me, I think."

"Running you hard, too, from the looks of it," Skiles said happily. "Come on in. I'll put coffee on."

Even though the day had lost little of its heat, coffee sounded like a good idea. Skiles led me through the entryway that doubled as his dining room and into his kitchen. It was large, as his rooms went, running almost the width of his house. The kitchen had two points of interest, both stoves. They were set asymmetrically against the back wall, a black, evil-looking, cast-iron monster in the center of the room and a shiny, new, gas range in the right hand corner.

"Had to have a gas bottle put in a while back," Skiles said as he lit a burner on the gas stove. "I'm getting pretty old for splitting and stacking and hauling wood."

I tapped the wood stove with the toe of my shoe. "You too sentimental to part with old Betsey?"

"No way to get it out," Skiles said with a rusty laugh that settled into a dry cough. "I built the house around it. Besides, I use it for heat in the winter. Grab yourself a seat. I'll just be a minute."

I sat down next to a screened window and watched as he poured water from a pail into a battered aluminium coffeepot and then spooned coffee into its basket. "That old stove fits my persona better anyway," Skiles said as he placed the assembled pot on a burner. "What you left of my persona, that is. Most of the pine people in this part of the woods know I'm an old fake by now."

"How do they feel about that?" I asked.

"Oh, they don't seem to mind. Most of them are flattered to think that an outsider would want to take up their way of life. That's the secret behind the welcome you'll get in most small towns and backwaters in this old world. City folks are different. They see their way of life as nothing more than their way of making money, and they don't want competition. Some for you, less for me, that kind of thinking."

Skiles climbed onto a tall stool and hooked his feet behind one of its rungs. "You better talk for a bit,

Owen. You'll be asleep elsewise. Tell me about the mystery that's running you to earth.''

"There are two mysteries," I said. "I've gotten more efficient since I saw you last. I can screw up two at once now.''

"I'm always in the market for new stories. Trot them out for me.''

I hadn't forgotten my original reason for visiting Skiles, but it no longer seemed as important as telling him what I had discovered. To the accompaniment of an angry fly at the window screen and the bubbling coffeepot, I began to relate the complete history of my adventures in Spring Lake.

I led off with Harry's story. Skiles nodded encouragingly as I touched off the various points of evidence, but he sat still and staring when I revealed the secret of Harry's sad business.

"There's no bottom to a human being," Skiles said, pulling at his chin in sad amazement. He brightened visibly when I described how Harry had knocked me down. "Nice to know you haven't changed," he said. "Still walking into trouble with your eyes open and your jaw out. So what are you going to do next?''

"Resign," I said. "First thing Tuesday morning when I can get in touch with Harry's folks. I've gone on as long as I can.''

"This Mary," Skiles said while pretending to study the coffeepot. "What was she to you?''

"An old friend," I said. "Why?''

"Excuse my nosiness, but I've been a storyteller long enough to know the difference between a man who's telling a tale from the outside looking in and one who's sitting in the middle peering out. You're in this story, son. The way your voice gets when you talk about this Mary makes me think you haven't quite got to the heart of it yet.''

When I didn't answer, Skiles got up and poured the coffee into surprisingly delicate, dark blue cups that would have fit in perfectly at the Gascony Inn. "Brought these from Philadelphia," he explained. "They're the last of their tribe. So how did you leave your friend Harry?"

"He was drawing a picture of Mary," I said, answering the literal question.

"That could be good or bad," Skiles said thoughtfully. "If he's got art in his blood, it could be his way of unloading his sorrow."

"How could it be bad?"

"Could just be more wallowing in the past. Bad for anybody." He was speaking from his own experience, as we both understood.

I tasted my coffee. It had a strange, bitter flavor.

"Chickory," Skiles said in reply to my expression. "Once you get used to it, plain coffee tastes like dishwater. Drink up and tell me about your other mystery."

Diana Lord's story came out more easily than Harry's had, which may have meant that telling it to Skiles was the real point of my visit. That Skiles was a good listener was to be expected of a man who had collected so many stories, but he was also a good audience. He stayed his coffee cup an inch from his lips when I described how Diana had disappeared into the lake. He held it there until I told him of the divers' unsuccessful search. Then he drank deeply. When I related the two versions of Brigid Kelly's unhappy history, Skiles nodded approvingly.

He stood up to refill my empty cup. "I'm inclined to agree with that police lady," he said. "I think she's right about this Diana Lord spinning a tall one for you and the priest."

"Why?"

"Because Diana fell so hard for the story of the drowned girl. And because she fell for the wrong version, the romantic one, the made-up one. It's been my experience that people who weave tales for others are the most likely to believe in whoppers themselves. I'm speaking as a professional here, Owen." He stood up straight and snapped one red suspender with his thumb. "So you can take this as gospel. A real storyteller knows a fiction from a truth instinctively. But a soul who lives in fantasies can't tell a lie from a barber pole. The fantasies are more real to them than the everyday world, you see. They want them to be true. So when they happen across another person's fantasy, they grab it and hold it to their hearts."

"Then I've been following a false trail," I said, thinking of my hope that Brigid's story would give me some insight into Diana's past.

"Hard to say for certain. There's no waste in the crazy business you've gotten yourself in, son. Everything's grist for your mill."

That "mill" was barely turning now. "I'd better be going," I said. "I want to get back before dark."

We both smiled at that, remembering how Skiles had once stranded me in this same forest as night had come on.

"Sure there isn't anything else you want to talk about?" Skiles asked.

He was still fishing for the story of Owen and Mary, but I wouldn't rise to the bait. "There is something else," I said. "I'm trying to track down a poem. It reminded Harry's mother of his problem. I'd like to know why."

"What's the name of this poem?"

"She couldn't remember the name or the poet, only that it was about a bird and the ocean."

"A bird and the ocean," Skiles repeated. "And a clue to a man pining away for his dead wife. By golly, I know that poem. It's right on the top of my tired old brain." He stared at the bare floorboards for a time, humming softly to himself. When he looked up, he was smiling. "Uncle Walt," he said. "You just wait here, Owen."

I studied the patch of sandy floor that had inspired Skiles without deciphering its message. My eyes were starting to close when the old man shuffled back in, carrying a fat book. He held the book open, and he was thumbing through it as he walked. I could read its title in worn gold lettering: *Leaves of Grass* by Walt Whitman.

"Here you go," Skiles said. "'Out of the Cradle Endlessly Rocking.' If this isn't the poem you're after, I'll burn my diploma. You have your own copy of this, I bet."

"No," I said.

"You don't have a copy of *Leaves of Grass?*" Skiles was plainly dumbstruck. "I can't imagine that. Going through life without this book would be like setting off through a desert without a canteen. What's wrong with you young people anyhow?"

The question reminded me of Sister Theresa's lecture. "Chrome," I said.

Skiles grunted. "I suppose that means something in some language." He held the book out to me. "Take mine," he said.

"Thanks, but I'll find a copy somewhere."

"Not before your Tuesday morning deadline you won't. Take it. The answer may be in there. Won't hurt you to read a few lines in any case. It's just a loan, mind you. Bring old Walt back someday and tell me how your two stories turned out. They're no good to me without endings."

I took the book and led the way back out through the front of the house. Skiles stopped on the cinder block front steps. "If I'm not here when you get back, you keep the book as a souvenir," he said.

"Where else would you be?" I asked.

"Well, I might just be exploring some of those deep, dark mysteries that eat at a certain Owen Keane so much. A man can't live forever, you know."

Standing in front of his weathered house in his baggy clothes, the old man looked as though he already had lived forever. He'd certainly learned more in this one lonely spot than I had in all my wanderings.

"I'll be back," I said.

TWENTY-TWO

SKILES'S COFFEE got me back to Spring Lake in one piece. I stopped to buy a bag of dinner at an old-fashioned drive-in just outside of town. A genuine car-hop brought out a tray to hang on the door of the Chevy, but I ungratefully ordered my burgers and root beer to go. I'd underestimated the staying power of a summer day; it was still light when I pulled into the Gascony's gravel lot. The light was a useless gray, though, that had faded to purple out over the ocean, and the streetlights had come on to embarrass it. I carried my dinner and the Whitman book to a quiet corner of the inn's porch that was lit by a living-room window.

I'd depended on the kindness of strangers all day for my meals, and the result had been a croissant and several cups of coffee. I had the thin, cold hamburgers eaten almost before I'd gotten Skiles's book open to the right page. Not that I searched the book with much enthusiasm. I had looked for clues in poems before in my checkered career and found them to be unreliable. It wasn't that I couldn't find what I was looking for; it was that I almost always found it, a circumstance that made me think that poems might be the police informants of literature, telling me anything I wanted to hear. My hesitation was also due to the feeling that this last, silly gesture would really finish my investigation of Harry's mystery and make my failure complete. I'd executed his father's commission and worked out the riddle of Harry's behavior, but I hadn't solved his mystery. I knew I had failed, because my answers hadn't brought Harry any peace.

I was still stalling when George Metelis slipped out through the darkened French doors of the breakfast room. "Thought it was you I saw out here," he said. He spoke quietly and stood a few yards away from me, a combination that made him hard to understand. "We've been hearing a lot about you this afternoon," Metelis added.

So the word was finally out. Pat O'Malia had done a remarkable job of keeping the lid on Diana's disappearance, but even she couldn't order back the Spring Lake tide. "Do you want me out of your inn?" I asked.

"No," Metelis said with enough hesitation to reverse the word's polarity. "Not before you're ready."

"I'll be ready soon. I need a place to sleep tonight, if that's okay."

"Of course," Metelis said, gracious in his relief. "I just thought I should warn you about the other guests." He nodded toward the window behind me. "Didn't want them to embarrass you."

Or vice versa, I thought. "Thanks," I said.

"And I have this for you. Shelly picked it up at the drugstore." He walked over and handed me a packet of photographs that I had taken during the week with my surveillance Nikon.

Good old Shelly, I thought. Still swinging away when the game was long past winning. If we'd been on better terms, Metelis might have grumbled at the way I had acquired the assistance of his waitress. I missed his complaining enough to paraphrase it now myself.

"I'm through commandeering your employees," I said, "and your office."

Metelis waved that half-apology away. Now that he finally knew my secrets, my landlord seemed saddened by them. That was often the way with mysteries, a lesson I had to learn over and over again. "Good night," Metelis said.

He left me alone on the porch, and I finally turned my attention to "Uncle Walt." My undergraduate experience with Whitman had left me with mixed feelings. About the time I'd arrived in college, the nineteenth-century poet had been adopted as an early flower child, and his reputation had soared. But I'd found too many of his longer poems to be windy, unedited catalogues of his world, clues piled up endlessly for someone else to winnow down.

"Out of the Cradle Endlessly Rocking" started in this characteristic way, the poet taking over twenty lines to introduce his "reminiscence." It was set on the "sands and the fields beyond, where the child leaving his bed wandered alone," its source the "memories of the bird that chanted to me/From your memories sad brother," and the response of the boy's "heart never to cease,/From the myriad thence-arous'd words." From his memories of this childhood experience, the poet, "chanter of pains and joys, uniter of here and hereafter," constructed his reminiscence. This conclusion to the introduction was promising. Certainly a man who could unite the here and the hereafter was just the person I was looking for. There was also something familiar and encouraging in the companion image, which told of the poet "Taking all hints to use them, but swiftly leaping beyond them." The line reminded me of Skiles's remark about everything being grist for my mill.

"You're a detective, Walt," I said softly. "And this poem of yours is a mystery story."

The bird made its entrance in the poem's next section. Actually, there were two birds, "Two feather'd guests from Alabama, two together." Whitman passed over their happiness with uncharacteristic brevity: *"Pour down your warmth, great sun! / While we bask, we two together."* Then he moved on to darker matters. "May-be kill'd, unknown to her mate, / One forenoon the she-bird crouch'd not on the nest, Nor return'd that afternoon, nor the next, / Nor ever appear'd again."

The poem then described at length the song of the "remaining one, the he-bird" listened to and preserved by the boy. The song began as a call to his mate, but it grew into an appeal to the universe to find and send back the lost love. At first I heard echoes of my own loneliness in this description, but then my grief seemed left behind by images that suggested only Harry: *"I am almost sure I see her dimly whichever way I look. / O rising stars! / Perhaps the one I want so much will rise, will rise with some of you."*

The bird's "aria" ended in words written for my friend: *"O past! / O happy life! O songs of joy! / In the air, in the woods, over fields, / Loved! loved! loved! loved! / But my mate no more, no more with me! / We two together no more."*

I set the poem aside half-finished and opened the packet of photographs that Metelis had left with me. In the sequence of pictures I'd taken of Harry's walk with Father Peter, I saw a face that perfectly matched

the bird's desperate song, the face of a sleeper struggling to wake from a terrible dream.

Then, as I flipped through the remainder of the
photographs, I came to a totally different face, Diana
Lord's. I had forgotten that I'd stolen a picture of her.
In the print I now held, she was lifting her face to
catch the sun, and her expression was as unmarked
and untroubled as any child's. Seeing her increased my
identification with the Whitman poem in ways I didn't
like. I slipped the prints back into their envelope and
hid it and the book of poems behind my wicker chair's
fat cushion.

There was one more job to do before I took advantage of George Metelis's hospitality for the last time.
I'd decided to check in on Harry, in the safe, secret
way I'd worked out earlier, by listening to his evening
concert.

Harry must have opened his windows to catch the
evening breeze; I could hear his clarinet faintly while
I was still a block away from the lake. I was weaving
my way along the same route Diana had used on her
escape, less than twenty-four hours before. Since then,
I'd told her story and Harry's over and over and listened to other stories told to me by Pat O'Malia and
Father Peter and Claire Dial and sister Theresa. I had
even heard the first part of a tale by Walt Whitman.
And I'd come to believe that all these stories were related somehow, if only because they all ran through
this one small town. It may have been that they were
only related because they all ran through my own small
head.

Spring Lake was busier now than it usually was at
noon, its paths taken by walkers and joggers and its
benches and banks by quiet couples. I sat down on a

bench across the lake from Harry's cottage and listened to his music for a while. His selection was the same bluesy piece that he'd been exploring earlier in the week. He'd worked out his problems with it since, and now he played slow, confident variations, each slightly different but all related, like the stories I'd collected in the course of my long day.

I was starting to doze off when someone behind me called out, "Hello."

It was Pat O'Malia, coming down the lighted path that ran behind my bench. Spring Lake's public safety director had traded her business suit for a tan slacks outfit that was still oddly formal. She was walking two large dogs, or rather, they were walking her. They were the brown, curly-haired giants I'd seen pictured in her office.

"Are you watching over your friend or waiting for the lady of the lake?" O'Malia asked as she came up to me.

I thought about it for a moment and drew a blank. "I don't know," I said.

She sat down on the bench beside me, and one of her dogs gave me the once-over with a wet nose. I drew my hands back and tucked my feet under the bench.

"Don't like dogs, Mr. Keane?" O'Malia asked.

"Not when they're big enough to saddle."

She laughed. "These two freeloaders are Irish water spaniels, a weakness of mine. This one is Nora, and the inquisitive one is Nick. I'm sure I don't have to explain those literary references to an old gumshoe like you. They'd rather be splashing in the lake than walking around it. They swim like fish. If you'd had this pair with you this morning, your lady friend would never have given you the slip."

I ignored that cheerful observation. "Have you had any luck tracing Diana?" I asked.

"No," O'Malia said, her cheerfulness suddenly much diminished. "She's given me the slip, too."

We listened to Harry's music for a few minutes. Then O'Malia said, "I'm going to have to talk with him about his recitals. He can't go on serenading his neighbors all night. This isn't Greenwich Village."

"Don't stop him yet," I said. "Please."

O'Malia sighed. "Are you hoping this is some kind of therapy?" When I didn't answer, she asked, "What's that he's playing now?"

I thought of the Whitman poem and his description of the bird's hopeless song. "Reckless, despairing carols," I said.

"I thought you were resigning from this case."

"I tried to. Harry's folks are away until Tuesday."

"So you're on duty till then?"

"Sort of," I said. "I've asked Father Peter to look after Harry."

"I wouldn't expect too much help from Peter Marruca. I've heard unofficially that he's leaving Spring Lake." She turned away from me and began to ruffle Nora's curly main aggressively. "It's his own idea, and a good one."

"It isn't Father Peter's idea." I spoke with a rare feeling of certainty, too tired to critically examine the idea that had suddenly popped into my head. "He's being forced out, blackmailed because he let himself get mixed up with Diana Lord."

"Forced out by whom?" O'Malia asked evenly.

"Your friend Helen Glass for one. I caught her putting the screws to him earlier today."

"Do you have any proof?"

"I don't need proof," I said. "I'm an amateur detective, remember? I just observe things that eventually click into place, usually right before the last commercial break."

O'Malia ignored the lip. "You're wrong this time," she said. "Nobody's running any priests out of Spring Lake. I wouldn't stand for it."

As near as I could tell in the darkness, she was looking me square in the eye. "Will you at least look into it?" I asked.

"Yes," she said. "Now do yourself a favor and get some sleep. I'll keep an eye on Mr. Ohlman until his family comes to claim him."

"It's a deal," I said.

TWENTY-THREE

I SLEPT LONG and soundly, without bad dreams or midnight visitors, and woke at ten Monday morning to the sound of a lawn mower parading back and forth beneath my window. A plan had sprung up in my head sometime during the night, its seed planted the evening before when I'd stumbled across the photograph of Diana Lord. I was through chasing legends and ghosts. I would act like a real detective for a change, and track down a living human being. Diana's photograph, combined with something I had observed at her house, gave me a slim lead. But it was a real lead this time, a real chance and maybe my last one.

I showered and dressed in the suit and tie that Mr. Ohlman hadn't liked. Then I slipped out of the old inn without my free breakfast and without settling up with Metelis. I didn't want to give up my local base until I had permanently passed Harry off to his parents the next day. It was safe enough until then to leave him drinking and sketching under O'Malia's all-seeing eye. My guilty conscience flared up at the thought of fleeing my post yet again, but I placated it by taking Skiles's *Leaves of Grass* with me. If I had a quiet moment during the day, I'd finish the Whitman poem and be done with even the incidentals of Harry's case.

I drove a block away from the inn before stopping to check the road map I'd bought the day before. The clue I'd found at Diana's house, the one that made her photograph useful, was the college emblem I'd seen pasted on the top of her battered stereo. The sticker had actually carried the crest of a university: Drew. I thought the school was near New Brunswick, but I was wrong. I finally found it an inch or two further north on the map, in Madison.

As I drove north, retracing the route I'd traveled earlier in the week, it occurred to me that I'd be near enough to the Morristown area to justify a visit to Mary's grave. I'd been in Morristown itself on Thursday, and I had somehow managed to avoid the cemetery, but now the gesture seemed more important. Among the mysteries I hadn't solved in Spring Lake was the puzzle of one part of my reaction to Mary's death—the resentment of Harry, the survivor—that had almost kept me off the case entirely and, by killing off my sympathy for Harry, had made me slow to realize the truth about his strange mourning. I'd spent a good part of the last few days not thinking about my own feelings for Mary. I'd rejected Father Peter's accusation that I still carried a torch for her, passed on the chance to tell Edward Hennix about my own "unfinished business," and let Harry chase me off with some old story about Mary and my days at the seminary.

I thought now of a visit Mary had made to me back in that lost time. She'd traveled all the way to the little town in southern Indiana where St. Aelred's and I had lain hidden in green rolling hills. She'd come all that way to talk with me, to tell me about her plans with Harry. I'd involved her instead in my search for a missing seminarian, spoiling what should have been our last, long heart-to-heart. Solving that Indiana mystery had been so important to me at the time, that I'd let a larger question pass unnoticed. Namely, should I ever have let Mary go? Father Peter had phrased it differently: Had I ever really let her go? I arrived in Madison long before I'd puzzled out an answer to that.

Madison was an old town of shady streets surrounded by the urban sprawl that chokes most of northeastern New Jersey. With its solid, squat homes and tall trees, it could have been any college town in any sleepy corner of the country, except that it was ringed by strip malls and filling stations instead of cornfields and forests.

I realized just how slim my chances of tracing Diana were when I got to Drew University itself. The campus was compact enough, like the town it bordered, new buildings jammed in between old ones to create solid blocks of university, but it was also largely deserted. The student body I'd hoped to canvass was off sunning itself somewhere else this July morning. I convinced myself that this was an advantage, because it would allow me to concentrate on the faculty and staff. I started by visiting the registrar's office, where I established that there was no Diana Lord enrolled at Drew. I didn't let that discourage me, either. I told myself that it was just a confirmation of O'Malia's guess that Diana was using an alias. Then I really got to work, the kind of boring, routine, uninteresting work that real detectives do. I presented myself before each departmental secretary in turn, flashing the dubious credentials given to me by Harry's father for quite a different purpose and showing Diana's picture. The results were sometimes polite, but always negative.

I'd worked my way through most of the curriculum without success when I found myself standing in front of the student athletic center. There I belatedly remembered another fragment of information Diana had given me. She'd told me that she swam every night. That she always had. There can't always have been a haunted lake available for that, I reasoned. That had to mean a pool.

The inside of the athletic center was encouragingly humid and rank with chlorine. The student working the front desk put down his textbook and stared at the picture of Diana long enough to wear out his eyeglasses.

"There's no test later," I said.

"Sorry." He handed the photograph back. "I haven't seen her before. I'd remember." he tapped the name Diana Lord into the computer terminal on his desk for luck and read the result: "No match."

"Are there any other health clubs in the area?" I asked. "Any that might have pools?"

"Tons," the kid said.

He was all too right. The strip mall jungle that encroached on Madison and the campus was lousy with health clubs, judging from the list I gleaned from a phone-booth yellow pages. I stopped for a fast, bad lunch and then plunged on, visiting a YWCA and four private clubs with catchy names like Trimline and Former Self. The fifth club I visited had an ordinary name, Glen's Spa and Racquet Club, and a huge, old building that needed paint. It also had two pools, one inside and one out.

The front door opened onto a raised reception area that overlooked lighted tennis courts. There were exercise machines to the right of the courts. On the left, just inside the door, were racks of tennis equipment and clothes, fronted by a long counter. The woman behind the counter wore a white tennis outfit with the name "Midge" embroidered in script over the pocket of her shirt. She was plump and more tanned than Diana and as blonde as anyone I'd ever met.

I expected her broad smile to fade when she realized I wasn't a customer, but it beamed on steadily. "An investigator?" she asked, repeating the euphemism of the day. "No kidding. I took you for an insurance salesman." She glanced at Diana's picture. "So what do you want her for?"

"I can't say," I replied, by which I meant that I had no very clear idea. "She sometimes uses the name Diana Lord," I added.

Midge sniffed, "*Diana's* right, but not *Lord*."

"You know her?"

"I might," she said, smiling coyly. A full minute passed. Then she beckoned me closer. I leaned across the counter, coming close enough to identify her gum as spearmint. "Isn't this where the detective reaches for his wallet?" Midge asked.

"One of us has been reading too many paperbacks," I said.

"Both of us, bud, but let's keep this on a business footing."

I glanced around. There was only one tennis player. He was taking a beating from a practice machine on the center court. The weight lifters were sweating it out in a distant corner of the cavernous room.

I took one of Mr. Ohlman's twenties out of my wallet and folded it up. I held it flat on the counter under the tips of my fingers. "How's that?" I asked.

"Better. The girl's name is *Cory*. Diana Cory. My guess is you're after her because she owes somebody some money. All I can say is good luck getting it back.

She's been a member here for two years, and she's never been current once."

"If she's a member, you must have an address," I said. "And no, this isn't where the detective reaches for his wallet again."

Midge laughed. "Just showing you the ropes, bud." She pulled open a drawer and ran her thumb along a card file. "96 Shelby Street. It's out the front door and about two miles south, and that's all you're getting for your twenty."

I slid the bill across the counter. "Best one I ever spent," I said.

I had second thoughts about that when I turned onto Shelby Street. It was narrow and badly paved, without sidewalks or curbs. The homes along the street were small Cape Cods, the kind thrown up by the thousands after the Second World War. I was still clinging to the idea of Diana Lord, the unhappy rich girl, running away from an unpromising wedding, and I couldn't picture her in this setting. 96 was slightly less well-cared for than its neighbors. The name "Cory" was painted on the mailbox in chalky white letters.

Whatever doubts I had about Diana and Shelby Street were dispelled when the front door of the house finally opened to my repeated knocking. The woman who opened it was bent forward slightly as though she were shouldering a load. Her skin was taut and leathery and her short hair was a homogeneous dark brown. I could smell the liquor on her breath through the smoke of the cigarette she carried. In spite of all that, I knew she was Diana's mother. The wide, thin mouth, the large gray eyes, even the cowlick were the same. She was dressed as though to heighten the resemblance, in a tee shirt and cut-off shorts.

"Mrs. Cory?" I asked.

"Yes. What do you want?"

Something, maybe my insurance salesman façade, was making her wary. I dropped the role of investigator and adopted one that might have been just as illusory. "I'm a friend of Diana's," I said. "A neighbor of hers from down at the shore. She left town suddenly. I didn't get a chance to say good-bye. I'm trying to find out if she's okay."

"Damned if I know that," Mrs. Cory said. "And as far as saying good-bye goes, don't hold out too much hope. Diana's never given me a good-bye. I just wake up, and she's gone. Like this morning.'

"Diana was here last night?"

"Yes. Came by after supper looking for a place to sleep. Didn't have anywhere else to go. End of the world. It's always the end of the world with Diana. You want to come in?"

I followed her into the small, cluttered front room of the house. It was almost filled by a baby grand piano, an ancient one, its varnish crisscrossed by fine cracks that gave its surface the look of alligator skin in the afternoon light.

"Do you play?" Mrs. Cory asked in response to my inspection. "I used to," she said. As she spoke, she gathered newspapers from the cushions of a couch. "Have a seat. Too early for a drink?"

"The sun's over the yardarm," I said, borrowing one of Metelis's salty expressions.

"Ginger ale highball okay? I'll be right back."

I found Diana everywhere I looked in the room. Diana as a baby in a silver frame on the piano. Ten-year-old Diana on a dock holding a fish in one half of a folding wooden frame at my elbow. The other half of the frame contained a slightly older Diana, perhaps thirteen, dressed for a party. I stood to examine a more recent photo that shared an end table with Mrs. Cory's overworked ash tray. It must have been Diana's high school graduation picture, still standing in the paper folder the photographer had provided. The young woman in the photograph was the Diana I had met, an unsmiling stranger among the earlier, happier portraits.

Mrs. Cory returned, carrying our drinks. I deduced from their color that she was rationing her ginger ale.

"Happy days," she said before drinking. "So you met Diana down at the shore. I thought she'd been getting too much sun. I've told her about that, but she never listens. Try to save a kid some of the knocks, it's a waste of your time. But wait until they need something." She winked at me. "Then stand back."

She took another long drink without removing her eyes from me. "Take Diana and me, for instance. I don't get so much as a phone call from her in months. She's shaken the dust of this place from her heels. She's gonna go to college. She's gonna marry a millionaire." Mrs. Cory scored the various points of Diana's program by rattling the ice in her now-empty glass. "She's gonna win the lottery, too, I suppose. Or the Irish sweepstakes."

"Might Diana have become engaged in the time she's been gone?" I asked, still clinging stubbornly to the story she'd told Father Peter.

"If she was, I didn't get my shower invitation. I wouldn't waste my worry on that, if I was you. Just Diana's standard moonshine, sounds like."

"Did she tell you where she's been these past months?"

"No. I heard that she was sharing a house up in Madison proper with some girls. I didn't know about this shore gig. I told her she was lucky to have a home to come back to." Mrs. Cory paused to light a cigarette. "Not that she was in the mood to talk last night. It was end of the world time, like I said. No point in talking at the end of the world."

"Would her father know where she is now?"

"He's in Rahway," she said, naming a nearby town. "We've been divorced for years."

"This house Diana shared in Madison. Do you know the address?"

"You look okay," she replied, shifting the subject slightly. "Get you another drink?"

"No thanks."

"What's your interest in Diana? Besides the usual, I mean."

"I think she's in trouble. I think you're right about it being the end of the world for her. I want to help her if I can."

"You got it bad, kid. I told you that doom and gloom was just part of her moonshine. I'd forget her if I was you. She'd never fall for anybody good for her, any more than she'd stay out of the sun. She's in for all the same knocks I've taken. That's just the way of the world."

She sucked on the ice in her glass. "That house she was sharing, I don't know the address, but it was supposed to be next to a supermarket at the edge of the campus. An A&P."

"Thanks," I said, standing.

"Good luck, kid. You're going to need it before this is over."

TWENTY-FOUR

ONE OF THE DANGERS of poking around like a real detective is that you find out things you'd just as soon not know. Witnesses contradict one another, and people you trusted don't pan out. Mrs. Cory had knocked the last prop from under my idealized vision of Diana. The embarrassment I felt now at having been taken in was like an old friend showing up at my front door with a suitcase in each hand. I knew it would be a long stay.

I was able to get directions to the A&P without any trouble. It was across the street from an old neighborhood that was being eaten away by the commercial sprawl. I stopped at a Dutch colonial home that seemed to be retaining its dignity despite its proximity to the supermarket and its attendant shops. There I met a man as old, almost, as Sister Theresa. He listened with one hand cupped behind his ear while I described the house I was after. "Two doors down," he said, waving his thumb to my right.

I followed the old man's thumb and found a house so added onto that the original shape of the structure was completely disguised. It was also overgrown by what might once have been ornamental trees and shrubs but were now shaggy monsters obscuring the lower-story windows and overhanging the front walk. I ducked beneath a shapeless dogwood to gain the moss green front porch and rang the bell.

This time, the person who answered was the right age. She was black and petite and not greatly taken with me. "We don't need any," she said, closing the door so quickly that it never came to rest after opening. I only had time to say two words, "Diana Cory," before the door shut, but they turned out to be the right two. After a moment, the door opened again, this time more slowly.

"Are you Paul?" the woman asked, using the name I'd seen on the card in Diana's room. She was wearing cutoffs, like Mrs. Cory, and a loose, pale green top that belonged in an operating room. There was a dish towel draped over one of her shoulders.

"My name is Owen Keane," I said. "I'm a friend of Diana's. I'm trying to find her." I added the vague statement that had become Diana's theme for me: "I think she's in some kind of trouble."

"Damn right she is," the woman said, thrusting her head toward me. "She's the only one who doesn't seem to know it. Turned up here yesterday like nothing ever happened. Like we're going to hug her and tell her how much we missed her. I called the police, so they could come and spell it out for her, but she got away before they showed up."

"What did Diana do?" I asked.

"She stole from us," the woman said, shifting from anger to exasperation in four short words. "Stole everything we've been saving, tuition money, rent money, food money."

"I don't believe it," I said.

"I don't give a damn what you believe, Owen Keane." She had pulled the towel from her shoulder, and she held it out before her now, stretched between two fists. "If you're a friend of Diana's, you probably believe in fairy tales. You may even be out of a fairy tale, like this Prince Charming of hers, this Paul. Diana's going to get our five thousand dollars back from him, if we all live long enough."

We stood staring at each other for a moment. My poker face must have been slipping, because she said, "You're not out of a fairy tale. You bought into one, didn't you? Diana ripped you off, didn't she?"

When I didn't answer, she began to close the door again. "Go cry it off somewhere else, Owen Keane," she said as the door swung shut. "We've got our own troubles."

I stood there for some time, trying to think of my next move. The answers I wanted were inside this jumbled, overgrown house, but I needed a way inside, a magic key from the fairy tale the woman had mentioned. Then I remembered that I had a key, a golden one.

I drove around Madison until I found a bank that advertised in its window the charge card that Harold Ohlman, Sr., had given me. The mid-afternoon lobby was almost deserted. That didn't keep the teller I chose from ignoring me while he counted out a stack of bills. When he finally granted me an audience, I produced the gold card. "I'd like a cash advance, please," I said.

"For how much?" the teller asked.

"For as much as I can get." That answer may have put him off, or perhaps my expectation that I could squeeze five thousand dollars from the tiny card was what Mrs. Cory had called "moonshine." After much telephoning, the branch manager agreed to give me a thousand.

I had time during the paperwork to reflect on the idea that I was robbing the firm of Ohlman, Pulsifer, and Hurst. But I had been doing that all along, by tracking Diana on the time I should have been spending on Harry. I had already greased one palm with money that wasn't mine. Now I planned to up the ante considerably.

Ten minutes later, I was back on the mossy front porch, leaning on the bell. The same young woman answered the door. "Look," she began.

"You look," I said. I waved a strap of twenties under her nose to give her looking material. "Here's a chance to recoup part of your losses. You get five hundred for letting me in to talk. When I've decided that we've talked long enough, you get another five."

"That's only a thousand," the woman said. "Diana stole five."

"Life's tough sometimes. What's your answer?"

She took the money and started back into the house. I followed her in, shutting the door behind me. She led me through a living room that reminded me of my own undergraduate days. There were cinder-block and board bookcases in one corner, and an old oriental rug served as a wall hanging. I paused to examine a mural painted in dark oils on the landlord's white wall. Its gray and brown geometric shapes suggested a scaffold awaiting a hangman.

"Who's the artist?" I asked.

"I am," the woman said. "Don't tell me you like it, or I'll have to paint it out."

We ended our walk in a dark kitchen, whose windows were blocked by shaggy old yews. A skillet of ground beef was browning on the range, and a stereo was playing softly. It was the battered portable I'd seen in Spring Lake. Diana had been here, all right.

The woman turned off the range and the stereo. Then she took a seat at one end of a phony butcher-block table. I took the chair at the opposite end, after placing the second strap of bills in the center of the table.

"What do you want to know?" the woman asked.

"Your name, for starters."

That request seemed to surprise her. "Vicky," she finally said.

"Vicky, when did you last see Diana?"

"Yesterday afternoon. Two o'clock, maybe. She was out of here, scared, by two minutes past."

Before she went to her mother's, I thought. I wouldn't learn where Diana was from Vicky, but there were other things I wanted to know. "How long have you known Diana?"

"A year or so. I met her at Drew."

"So she is enrolled there," I said.

"No. She worked there some and audited some classes. She told me that she wanted to enroll when she could get the money together. That was the first lie I fell for. The first of her big plans, I mean.

"I felt sorry for her. Her mother's a professional victim and her father's worse. You know about him?"

"Only that he lives in Rahway."

Vicky laughed at that. "Like he has a choice."

It took me a moment to interpret that strange remark. "Rahway prison?" I asked.

She nodded.

"What for?"

"Basic, traditional stuff. He steals things. Diana's made me a believer in heredity, I can tell you that. I used to think it was funny, the way Diana could pick any lock she saw. Then she spoiled the joke." We both looked down at the stack of bills, which was sitting in a circle of light cast by a hanging lamp. "But it wasn't really her old man she took after. He just added the vocational training. She's her mother's daughter, that's her big problem. Diana told me story after story about her mother. They're the only stories I still believe.

"Mrs. Cory is one old-fashioned, dependent person. Every rainbow has a man at the end of it, and every one's a bum, like her husband. Just having them come and go all the time was hard on Diana, but then she got old enough to interest them herself. She's had a rough few years. That's why I felt sorry enough for her to talk my roommates into taking her in. I wanted to get her out of that mess, which makes me a prize moron."

"Why?"

"Because we carry our own messes around with us, Owen Keane. Up here in our heads. And nobody can save us from those. Diana is as bad as her mother ever was. Mooning around, waiting for someone to save her—some man to save her—never thinking that she might have it in her to save somebody else. Dreaming up dreams that were never going to come true, watching old movies all day. I mean *old* ones, too. Black-and-white ones, and I'm not just talking about the film. They had black-and-white plots, too, where everybody's either all good or all bad and everything turns out all right in the end."

"Where people die for love," I said.

"Or love saves them, which is even less likely. That's what Diana is looking for, a love that will save her.

Something out of Metro-Goldwyn-Mayer, circa 1939."

That seemed to bring us back to the soiled card in Diana's Spring Lake room. "What do you know about Paul?" I asked.

"Not much. I thought you might be him, except for..." She hesitated and smiled for the first time.

"For my suit being too cheap?"

"Yes, sorry. Paul's loaded, according to legend. Diana started seeing him last fall. I mostly know what he's not like, which is not like the men Diana usually falls in with, the abusive losers. Paul's big attraction is that he's so different: gentle, thoughtful, caring."

Vicky stood up. "For a thousand bucks, you should get your pick of Diana's leavings. Maybe you can find yourself a memento."

She circled around behind me and opened a door. I listened to the sound of her footsteps descending an uncarpeted staircase while I studied the patterns in the table's artificial wood grain. The fatigue of the previous two days was returning, but this time it was entirely mental, a side effect of having had to rearrange all the facts I'd carefully stored away. I might just as well have saved myself the effort.

Vicky returned carrying a large cardboard box. She removed several long rolls of paper that had been sticking out of the top of the box so she could rummage around inside. Then she handed me a video cassette. "I can't believe Diana left that," she said. "It's one of her prized possessions."

I examined the tape. James Stewart and Donna Reed smiled at me from its cover. *"It's a Wonderful Life,"* I read aloud.

"They don't come any more hokey," Vicky said. "Here's another of the crown jewels." She handed me a small, green pillow embroidered with the seal I'd noticed on the old stereo, the crest of Drew University. "Diana would hug that like a teddy bear, the poor fool." Vicky's tone was softer now than her words. "It's as close to a diploma as she'll ever get.

"Talking about Paul reminded me of this stuff. One of the jobs Diana did around the campus was modeling for art classes. That's how I met her. Paul met her that way, too, in some evening school class. He gave her some of the sketches he did of her. Pretty mediocre stuff, really. Technically, they're all right. He's got some talent for exteriors, but as portraits of another human being, they're pretty shallow."

I unrolled the paper tube she handed me. The sketch was a nude of Diana, the unself-conscious, unconcerned Diana who had found her way into my room that first night. Seeing her again was the first of two blows that seemed to hit me within the span of a heartbeat. For I also knew the artist of the unsigned sketch. I recognized its slashing lines as the work of my unhappy friend, Harry Ohlman.

TWENTY-FIVE

IT WAS EARLY EVENING when I pulled into the All Souls Cemetery. I was the only visitor on the quiet hillside, apart from some small, sharp-winged birds that were darting down the rows of graves and through gaps in the headstones, hunting for something I couldn't see. I parked my car on a one-lane access road a few yards above Mary's grave and walked down to it, carrying flowers I'd purchased on the drive from Madison. I was also carrying Skiles's *Leaves of Grass,* like some out-of-date suitor who thought that flowers and poetry were the way to a woman's heart.

I had no business romancing this woman; her headstone made that clear enough. It was a large stone, with Mary's name set on the right-hand side of its broad face. The left was smooth and bare. "BE-LOVED WIFE AND MOTHER," it said beneath Mary's name. Despite what I'd learned that day, I knew that the first half of that claim, made by some sentimental stonecutter on Harry's behalf, was true enough.

"Hello, Mary," I said. I inserted the flowers in a metal vase set in the ground at the center of the stone. Then I sat down, off to one side, on new grass that was spiky and hard from the summer heat. I'd left my jacket in the Chevy, and I rolled up my sleeves now and loosened my tie.

"We have to talk," I said. "I mean, I wish to God we could." Beyond her grave, down in the valley at the foot of the hill, I could see the steeple of the little

wooden church where Mary's funeral had been held.
"Harry wasn't at your funeral," I said, thinking
aloud. "He was in the hospital. If he'd had to stand
here and watch them bury you, maybe none of this
would have happened. He would have faced it.
Maybe."

It occurred to me that I was giving a rambling report. I picked a buckthorn and considered its droop-
ing head while I organized my thoughts. Then I began
again. "I've been down in Spring Lake for the last two
weeks, watching Harry. You remember Spring Lake.
You spent a week there last summer. It must have been
a happy one, because Harry went to a lot of trouble to
recreate it. That memory had another attraction for
him, I now know. It was a time before his fall from
grace.

"While I was down there, I met a woman. That
would be a good beginning for a story. I thought of
her as being in another story entirely, the tale of a rich
girl running away from an arranged marriage, a girl
obsessed with death and memories. I was wrong. It
wasn't another story. It was part of the one I was supposed to be figuring out, a branch the story had taken
before I'd gotten involved.

"Harry's been pretending that you are still alive.
I've known that for a couple of days now. I decided
that it was his grief that drove him to that, but I was
wrong there, too. Guilt was mixed up with the grief.
More than one person's tried to tell me that, but I
couldn't make it fit in. I knew that Harry wasn't responsible for your death. It never occurred to me that
the guilt predated it, that the accident only made the
guilt permanent for Harry."

The sky above the little church was darkening. The only sound I could hear was hot ticking made by the Chevy behind me. I threw away the weed I held and picked another. "I remember now that you once joked with me about Harry playing around. At least I thought you were joking. If I'm guessing right, Harry did cheat on you last fall, with a young woman he met in an art class. He told her that his name was Paul—remember Paul Gauguin, the painter Harry always talked about at Boston?—and he sent her flowers. Probably charged them on his credit card, the dope. Maybe that's how she traced him, but I'm getting things out of order.

"Yesterday I spoke with an old nun. You would have liked her. She told me yet another story. The theme of this one was hopeless forgiveness. The story was about a woman who drowned herself because she decided her father couldn't forgive her and about a father whose life was destroyed because he couldn't forgive his drowned daughter. The nun was telling me Harry's story all over again, but I couldn't see it then, maybe because Harry's situation is reversed. The sinner is still alive in his case, and the forgiver is dead.

"You died before you could forgive Harry for betraying you. That's what's crushing him now. 'Unfinished business' someone else I've talked to called it, except that with Harry, it isn't some small regret that's eating at him. It's the knowledge that he turned his back on your marriage, that he betrayed the best thing in his life, that he's cut off from you now with no hope of mending the break.

"His despair of ever being forgiven by you is what drove him to recreate a happy time before he met this other woman. Then I blundered in, in my standard fashion. I discovered what he was doing, but not why. I thought his grief at losing you was enough of a motive. It would have been for me.

"I've missed you," I said. I stopped at that. It wasn't just that my voice was reluctant, suddenly, to go on. I was saddened by the uselessness of addressing the dumb block of stone. If it had been Mary before me, alive again, and not her headstone, telling her that I'd never gotten over her would have been just as pointless. Alive, she would have been with Harry, not me.

On my drive to Madison that morning, I'd begun to admit to myself the truth of what Father Peter and Skiles and Harry had all seen, that I had never gotten over losing Mary. Now I saw that the whole truth was even stranger than that. I'd never even admitted to myself that I had lost her. Somehow, down through the long years, I'd sheltered the belief that we would be together again someday, that we were meant to be. It was a delusion as thorough and sad as Harry's dream that his dead wife was still alive. The only difference between Harry and me was that I had seen Mary buried. I might kid myself that there was life for us after Harry Ohlman, but one trip to All Souls Cemetery had ended the dream. That was why I'd moved like a sleepwalker through the months since the funeral and why I'd resented Harry so much. I'd never get Mary back from him now.

"Another mystery solved," I said, my voice slowly coming to life again like a cold engine. "I begrudged Harry all those years he'd had with you. All the mornings he woke up beside you," I added, remembering the list of advantages that Harry had recited for me at our last meeting. "That you pushed him to be better than he was. I resented his knowing all the little details of your life and all your secrets. Your bad back, for instance. Harry called that 'the big secret.' Why? I'd known about it already. Somebody mentioned it to me recently." I reran the list of people I'd spoken with in the last two weeks. "Angela Nickelson, your friend from the school board, told me. She said you'd hurt your back when Amanda was born, that you'd been given medicine for it—pain-killers?— that you wouldn't take. Why was that such a big secret?"

There was no answer from the stone before me or from inside my head. I was stirring myself to leave, when my hand fell on the book of poetry.

"Maybe you can help me with this," I said. "It's a poem your mother-in-law set me onto, 'Out of the Cradle Endlessly Rocking,' by Walt Whitman. Remember how we used to help each other through the poetry classes at Boston? English Renaissance with D-minus Doherty and Romantic Poetry with Dr. Tavel? I had a crush on her. This poem should be straightforward in comparison. I've already read the first part. It's about the poet as a boy observing two nesting shorebirds. One of the birds disappears, and the survivor sings his heart out to her."

I began reading then by the fading light, not aloud as I'd intended; my one-sided banter had only depressed me, reminding me of Harry's hopeless pretense. The point where I took up my reading was another of Whitman's long lists. This one described the scene as the surviving bird's aria died away. Although the bird's notes echoed on for a time, their place in the foreground was taken by the "angry moans" of the ocean, "the fierce old mother." The boy was almost overcome by the bird's song and by the stirring of similar songs within him: "The love in his heart long pent, now loose, now at last tumultuously bursting." This emotion corresponded to the "undertone," the working of the same ocean I'd heard every day in Spring Lake, "incessantly crying" to the boy "some drown'd secret hissing/To the outsetting bard."

The boy/poet then challenged the bird, calling it a demon and asking whether its song was addressed to its mate "or is it really to me?" The song has awakened something inside the boy. "Now in a moment I know what I am for." Having heard the bird's song and understood it, and having felt the echo within of "a thousand songs, clearer, louder and more sorrowful than yours," the boy realized that his life has been changed forever. "Never more shall I escape, never more the reverberations . . . the sweet hell within,/The unknown want, the destiny of me."

The next line reminded me of my early guess that the poem was really a mystery story. "O give me the clew! (it lurks in the night . . .)." The poet was willing to settle for a single word, "The word final, superior to all." The thing addressed, the source of the word, was not the bird, but the ocean: "Are you whispering it, and have been all the time, you sea waves?" The sea answered, "Delaying not, hurrying not," by whispering to the poet "the low and delicious word death,/And again death, death, death, death."

Death again, I thought, my attention wandering away from the poem's last few lines. Like guilt, death had been a recurring theme in my investigation, although it had turned up more often in Diana's branch of the story than it had in Harry's. Her obsession with death was a piece that wouldn't fit now. Was it never more than the "doom and gloom" her mother had spoken of? If all of her stories had been lies, she had never been the desperate rich girl running away from some mysterious trouble, why was the fear I'd sensed in her so strong? Why was she so interested in Brigid's story? And why had she approached Father Peter with her questions about death and suicide?

To answer those questions, I had to remind myself why Diana had come to Spring Lake in the first place. The answer was Harry Ohlman. Harry was a Catholic; the Church's position on suicide would have meaning for him. Brigid Kelly was a suicide who had killed herself over lost love. That was the story Diana had believed. Could she have been afraid that Harry might take the same way out?

I stood up quickly and teetered on the hillside for a moment, off balance. "Mary had a bad back," I said, quoting Harry. Then I seemed to hear his hollow laughter.

TWENTY-SIX

I HAD TO GET BACK to Spring Lake. That simple idea suddenly seemed more important than any I'd had in months. Unfortunately, the rest of the world didn't share my sense of urgency. Traffic was heavy and slow on the winding two-lane into Morristown. It was fully dark when I crossed the intersection where Mary had died. Ten minutes later, I was in the town itself, passing within a couple of blocks of the cell where Mitchel Henry sat, smoking and thinking of his next drink. South of Madison, which I reached a slow thirty minutes later, Mrs. Cory might have been having a nightcap herself, or maybe she'd gotten a head start on sleeping off the day's work.

I'd kidded Pat O'Malia earlier about how the pieces of the mystery suddenly click into place for an amateur detective. But that was happening now for me, now that it might be too late. I thought of Edward Hennix's casual remark about widowed people having a high rate of suicide. I remembered Harry telling me that he had the rest of his life to get the portrait of his dead wife right, as though it was the last task he'd set for himself.

While stopped at a light in Chatham, I saw a phone booth on the corner of a gas station's lot. Harry didn't have a phone, but there were other possibilities. I first tried Father Peter at St. Brigid's rectory. I got the parish secretary, who told me that the priest was out and would not be back for hours. Next I dialed the

Spring Lake police department in search of Pat O'Malia.

"The director's gone home for the day," the policeman who answered told me. "Is this an emergency?"

"I don't know," I said, the stranger's bored voice making me question my own apprehension. I hung up on him and tried the home number printed on O'Malia's business card. For that effort, I got to speak to her answering machine. Somehow, her cheerful recording had a further dampening effect. "This is Owen Keane," I said, almost apologetically. "Please check in on Harry Ohlman as soon as possible."

I should have called the policeman back, but I'd begun to doubt in earnest my wild deduction that Harry meant to kill himself with Mary's unused medicine and that the sketch of his wife was really his suicide note, his simple explanation to the world.

I started out again, finally reaching the Garden State Parkway south of Newark half an hour later. I headed south at seventy miles an hour, weaving the Chevy in and out of traffic that was still perversely heavy at nine o'clock. As I drove, I spotted an exit for Rahway and thought of Diana's father. His influence explained her ability to suddenly appear in locked rooms, an explanation that dispelled what little remained of her mysterious aura. Traffic slowed down along a narrow stretch of the highway that squeezed through the buildup around South Amboy. The lines of trucks and buses finally began to thin out south of Matawan. I flew past the exit for Red Bank, where Harold Ohlman, Sr.'s, letter had found me in hiding. Finally, almost three hours after I'd struggled to my feet at

Mary's graveside, I pulled off the expressway and
headed east toward Spring Lake.

There were still a few strollers about at half past ten,
but the streets were empty and quiet. I parked in front
of Harry's cottage and ran the half-dozen yards to his
front door on stiff legs. There were no lights on inside. The windowless front door was locked. I tried the
door's brass knocker and then banged on the door
with my fist. The only answer was the yapping of the
neighbor's dog.

I circled the house as I'd done on my last visit,
looking in the black windows as I went. They were all
closed and locked. I mounted the back steps where I'd
last seen Harry, only the day before. Like the front
door, the back one was locked. This door had windows, though. A garbage can stood next to the back
porch steps. I took a paper grocery bag from it, shaking the bag empty of Harry's trash. Then I lay the bag
over the windowpane closest to the doorknob and
punched my hand through it. Harry hadn't set the
dead bolt; the door opened when I reached through
and turned the button on the knob.

There was no sound from inside the house in answer to my noisy entry. The air inside the kitchen was
stale and cool. I switched on the lights and saw that I
was alone in the room. I crunched across broken glass
to the dining and living rooms and found that they
were deserted, too. Then I hurried down the dark
hallway. The tiny bathroom was empty. Across the
hall, Harry's studio was a mess. The sketches I'd been
asked to admire on an earlier visit had been ripped
from the walls, and their fragments entirely covered
the floor. I registered the fact in the second it took me
to draw my hand back from the light switch. Then I

was moving again, toward the last room, Harry's room. In the few steps that remained, I realized that I should have started my search with this room. It surely had been Harry and Mary's bedroom during their happy visit the summer before, making it the single place in the whole house most sacred to Harry.

I stopped at the threshold of the room and reached inside for the wall switch. The harsh ceiling light revealed Harry, sprawled across the bed. His portrait of Mary lay next to him. On the floor beside the bed stood a half-empty bottle of scotch. Next to it on the floor was the thing I'd been imaging all through my long drive, a brown pill bottle. It was open and on its side.

Seeing the empty pill bottle lying there exactly as I'd imagined it and Harry beside it exactly as I'd pictured him seemed to give the whole scene the quality of an imagined thing, a dream I'd made up to frighten myself. I felt unsteady on my feet, as I had at the cemetery, and I landed against one side of the doorway heavily. "Too late," I said loudly as I caught myself. "Harry, goddamn it."

I almost fell again as Harry answered me by groaning faintly. I stumbled to the bedside and shook him by the front of his shirt, more as a release for me than as an attempt to revive him. I did revive him, though. His eyes opened and he read my last line back to me: "Owen, goddamn it."

I dropped him back onto the bed. "Are you all right?" I asked.

Harry didn't seem to be sure himself. I saw a mirror image now of my disoriented moment at the doorway. Harry squinted around the bright room as though it and I were parts of a dream. "What the hell?'' he asked. His voice was thick, and his eyes slid from shocked amazement to apathy as he spoke. His head was settling back on the pillow when I grabbed his shirt again.

"No you don't," I said, pulling him into a sitting position. "Get up. We're walking." We paced the room then, Harry dragging along with his arm around my shoulder as we caromed off walls and furniture. I talked to him until I got winded, questioning him and getting no answers for my trouble. Five minutes later his dead weight won out. I tried to sit him on the edge of the bed, but he slid down onto the floor. He was still upright, though, and his eyes were open.

Harry looked me over, critically. "Your hand's bleeding," he said.

I looked down and found that he was right. My right hand was bleeding freely. "I broke a window," I said.

Harry blinked at that. "What are you doing here bleeding?" he asked.

"Saving your life, I think." I bent with an effort and retrieved the empty pill bottle, which one of us had kicked under the dresser. It was Mary's prescription, as I'd guessed. "How many of these did you take?"

Harry seemed genuinely shocked by the suggestion. Then he made an effort to remember, running one hand through his thin hair in a pantomime of concentration. "None," he finally said. "I was just looking at them. I look at them every night."

"The pills are gone, Harry. You're alone in here. The place is locked up tight. What did you do with them?"

"I didn't take them," Harry said. "I tried to. I've tried for days. I couldn't." His crusty voice began to quit on him, as mine had at Mary's grave. "I couldn't," he managed to repeat.

He began sobbing then. I was too confused to console him. I paced the room unsteadily, thinking aloud. "You can't have taken them," I said. "You'd be out cold. But they're gone. You're alone in a locked house."

My second mention of locks finally registered with me. "Diana Cory." Harry's crying stopped abruptly when I spoke her name. I went on reciting guesses to myself, stringing them together. "She came back to Spring Lake. Hitchhiked back while I was in Madison. She had nowhere else to go. Her mother told me that. She said it was end-of-the-world time for Diana. Her friends had tried to have her arrested. Diana was going to get their money back from Paul. From you," I said, turning to Harry. "Was she here tonight?"

Harry didn't waste my time denying that he knew her. "I don't know if she was here," he said quietly. "I passed out."

"She got here after you passed out," I said, leaping beyond his testimony. "She found you here with the pill bottle and decided to save you. She took the pills away with her."

"Where?" Harry asked.

"Out there," I said, looking toward the darkness beyond the windows.

Harry surprised me for the second time by struggling to his feet. "We've got to find her, Owen," he said. "She has those pills. You said that she has nowhere to go, that it's the end of the world for her." His voice seemed to shed its numbness as he spoke. He took me by the shoulders as if I was the one who needed rousing. "Come on. We've got to find her before it's too late."

He headed off down the hallway, ricocheting from wall to wall as he gathered speed. We went out through the front door, Harry leading the way as far as the front steps. There he stopped short as though dazed by the night air. "Where?" he asked again.

I kept moving while I tried to think of an answer. Before us lay Spring Lake, the color of an old, dull nickel under an indifferent moon. Diana had run to the lake before to escape, on the night when she'd told me that she might go to be with Brigid.

I took off at a run across Lake Shore Drive with Harry coming up noisily beside me. It suddenly seemed to me like a scene from Boston College nineteen years before, the two of us playing Hardy Boys again, out to solve all the mysteries of the world. We were too old for that game now, and too beaten up. Harry was already limping by the time we reached the edge of the lake, and I was still a long step behind the action, struggling to figure it out.

The surface of the lake was smooth and undisturbed. I could see a silver-haired couple walking under a streetlight on the far bank and one or two others on widely scattered benches. A jogger startled us by thumping along the path behind us in the darkness.

"It's no good, Harry," I said. "There are too many people here. They would have scared her off." I looked toward the wooded northern shore, a black mass now in spite of the moon. "She could be anywhere, waiting for her chance. Or not waiting. We'll never find her."

Harry wouldn't let me give up. "Damn it, Owen, figure it out. You always figure it out."

I felt again that we'd been transported somehow back to Boston and the old days. I was on the trail of something important, and Harry was prodding me on. None of the terrible things that had happened since that time were real. None of the failures mattered. I could solve the mystery. I could know the answer. And suddenly, I did.

"Diana told me she might go to be with Brigid Kelly," I said.

"Who?" Harry asked.

"A woman who drowned in the lake years ago. I thought Diana meant that she was going to the lake herself. But Brigid isn't in the lake. She's in the church. She's buried there."

"Come on, then," Harry said, limping off without me.

I overtook him easily, running with measured strides, as I had the night I'd chased Diana to the lake. St. Brigid's was dark and deserted. I took its steep steps two at a time, finally slowing to a winded walk at the end of my climb. At the top of the stairs there were three pairs of bronze doors, all locked.

Harry was struggling up the stairs as I started down. "Wait at the top," I said.

There were still lights on in the rectory. I ignored the old mechanical bell and banged on the door, yelling Father Peter's name at the same time.

The priest appeared a moment later, fully dressed and angry. "What in God's name," he began.

"I need the keys to the church," I said. "Diana may be inside."

"The church has been locked all evening," Father Peter replied, confused.

"Not for her. Hurry, please."

He left me on the doorstep and returned a moment later, carrying a ring of keys and a flashlight. Harry was waiting as instructed on the top step. His wild appearance startled the priest. "What is all this?" Peter demanded.

"Unlock the door," Harry ordered, using a tone I hadn't heard since I'd left his law firm. "Hurry up."

The priest obeyed, handing Harry the flashlight and selecting the right key on the first try.

Then I was through the heavy door, leading the way across the soundproof vestibule and into the nave. Brigid's grave lay in the darkness to our right. The beam of Harry's flashlight beat us all into that dark corner. There it played across a motionless figure on the bare stone, Diana Cory.

I hesitated at the opening of the alcove as I had at the doorway to Harry's room. Harry brushed past me, followed by the priest. I watched as Harry knelt next to Diana. "She's still breathing, Owen," he called to me.

The priest, kneeling across from him, repeated the message. "She's still breathing."

TWENTY-SEVEN

ACCORDING TO a large clock on the wall before me, the sun should have been coming up, but I couldn't verify it from where I sat. The waiting area of the emergency room was windowless and very small. Fortunately, Harry and I had it to ourselves for the moment. Not that Harry was much company. He was currently stretched out on a row of armless vinyl chairs, sleeping soundlessly, oblivious to the soft elevator music and the infrequent public address announcements. I'd begun the vigil by pacing the tiny space like an expectant television father, but the noise of my steps on the bare linoleum had resounded like gunshots in the general stillness. I finally dropped into a chair instead as the night's nervous energy slowly leaked out of me like air out of yesterday's balloon.

I was almost asleep myself when Pat O'Malia entered the room. She was overdressed as always, this time in a pale gray suit and a rose-colored blouse. She carried two cups of vending-machine coffee.

"No croissants this morning," she said as she sat down. "No change on Diana from the last report," she added. "All the signs are good, but she's still not conscious. It's a lucky thing for her that she didn't mix those pills with alcohol, like your friend here was planning to do. How's the hand?"

I held up my right hand to display my bandaged knuckles.

"You'll have to sign up for lock-picking lessons from Ms. Lord."

"Cory."

"Right."

O'Malia had shown up at the hospital thirty minutes after the ambulance had carried Diana there. Since then O'Malia had bustled about, greeting the staff by name and giving me the impression that she was overseeing Diana's treatment personally. I decided that O'Malia was a morning person. An early morning person. She was her cheerful, friendly self again, her recent criticism of me and my work apparently forgotten.

O'Malia studied Harry for a time as he slept and then treated me to the same examination. "What's keeping you awake?" she finally asked.

"My underwear," I said, remembering one of her better insults. "I accidentally put it on backwards this morning."

She laughed loudly enough to cause Harry to stir slightly. "That's another thing I don't like about amateur detectives," she said. "They're all smart-asses."

"Sorry," I said.

"So am I. I was wrong about you, Mr. Keane. You did good." The admission seemed to embarrass her, and she blew noisily on her coffee before tasting it.

I was embarrassed myself, too embarrassed to let even a small compliment stand unqualified. "I was just wondering how much of this would even have happened if I hadn't wandered in," I said.

O'Malia shrugged off that imponderable. "Who knows? I still don't have that clear an idea about what actually did happen last night. Why don't you start at the top and give me the whole story. I promise to applaud at all the appropriate points."

I began by repeating the deductions I'd made the evening before at Mary's grave regarding Harry's infidelity with Diana Cory and his despair of ever being forgiven for it by his dead wife.

This dovetailed with the part of the story I'd told O'Malia two days earlier in her office, and she made the connection for me to demonstrate that she understood so far. "Harry Ohlman came here to Spring Lake because he'd been happy here with his wife before the business with Diana Cory," O'Malia said. "Pretending his wife was alive was as much a relief from guilt as it was from grief. But how did Diana come to follow him here? You said he gave her a phony name."

"I'm not sure how she traced him. If I know Harry, he told her everything when he broke it off. That would have made it easier for her. Somehow, though, she found him down here. She stole her roommates' savings to finance her own stay."

"To try to win Harry Ohlman back?"

"Her roommate Vicky told me that Diana was looking for someone to save her, never thinking that she had it in her to save someone else." I was speaking slowly now, puzzling it out for myself as I explained it to the policewoman. "Vicky was underestimating Diana Cory. I think that Diana was still hoping that Harry would rescue her from a life she hated, but she was worrying about Harry, too, and trying to protect him. She did save him in the end, after all."

"I'm not convinced of that," O'Malia said, "but we'll get back to it later. You haven't told me yet how you were able to trace Diana Cory when the best brain on the squad, meaning me, had come up empty."

I described how I'd tracked down Diana with her photograph and the college emblem, hoping that my ingenuity would impress the professional. Instead, it irritated her.

"A hundred-to-one shot," she said, shaking her head.

"You were right about Diana," I added to cheer O'Malia up. "She was spinning a fantasy for Father Peter and me. There were no wealthy parents and no wedding. I don't know where she came up with that tale. Her mother told me that Diana is always inventing happy futures for herself. Vicky said that Diana loves old movies—*It's a Wonderful Life* is her favorite—with black-and-white plots and miracle endings.

O'Malia was suddenly smiling brightly enough to interrupt me. "Don't you ever watch old movies?" she asked.

"Only ones with detectives in them," I said.

"I should have spotted it earlier. That wool Diana pulled over your eyes was secondhand. She lifted it from one of her old movies, *The Philadelphia Story*. She gave Helen Glass a Philly address, remember? And Lord was the last name of Katherine Hepburn's character, a rich girl who balks at a wedding in the last reel." O'Malia shook her head again, her good humor restored now by having fielded a ball that had passed between my legs. "What a world."

"Diana's story wasn't all moonshine," I said, borrowing Mrs. Cory's word. "Father Peter recognized, correctly, that Diana was preoccupied with death. And I saw fear in her eyes that she didn't lift from any old movie plot. The trouble was that I misread it. I assumed that she was thinking of her own death, and that she was afraid for herself. In fact, she was worried about Harry. She was attracted to Brigid Kelly's story because it echoed her movie fantasies, but there was more to it than that. I think the story was also important to Diana because it reminded her of Harry's situation. Dying for love was something Harry Ohlman might actually do, something that Diana wanted to prevent."

"You sound like you're describing two different women," O'Malia said.

"I know. That's really what I learned about her in Madison. There was the woman forced out of a broken home by her mother's boyfriends, the daughter apprentice of a thief. But there was also a romantic girl, dreaming of a way out and fooling herself with the dreams."

"You knew that before you went to Madison," O'Malia said. She had crumpled her empty coffee cup into a ball, which she now rolled between the palms of her hands. "You described her as naive and cynical the first time we talked."

"I saw it then, but I didn't understand it. I also saw that Diana was close to the end of her rope, but I didn't know why. I was still thinking of her as an unhappy debutante, running away from the altar. But she was really afraid that she was failing with Harry. She told me once that she was thinking of giving up, of becoming a memory. I thought she was referring to Brigid, but now I think it was Mary Ohlman. Diana was tired of trying to fight Harry's memories of Mary.

"Harry had to completely ignore Diana when she showed up here; otherwise, his fantasy wouldn't work. He was here with Mary, and the world was fine. He hadn't even met Diana yet. She and the accident were both in a future that Harry never intended to reach.

"His attitude must have totally mystified Diana, but she stuck to him. She must have been disturbed by what she saw him doing, just as I was. She played a waiting game, approaching Father Peter when she saw him looking after Harry. Later, when I showed up and Diana saw me leaving Harry's cottage, she came to see me. In both cases, she was just trying to stay in contact with Harry." I secretly hoped that I was wrong in this one particular, that Diana had had other reasons for coming to me. I looked over at O'Malia to see if she had detected that foolishness in my voice, but she was chewing on something else.

"Speaking of Peter Marruca, you were right about Helen Glass and her cronies pressuring him to resign," O'Malia said. "I did some checking. Then I did some head knocking. I went to speak with Father Peter yesterday myself, to apologize for the town. I couldn't talk him out of leaving."

"He saw Diana as a test he had failed," I said. "But he might be thinking differently about it this morning. He was right about one thing: the idea that all the stories in Spring Lake were tangled together. That was the key to the mystery—not that the stories were tangled, but that they were really all part of one story.

"I thought that I was the reason Harry went on a drinking binge the night Diana disappeared, and that Diana's showing up in my room that night when I had my hands full with Harry's troubles was just an unlucky coincidence. I'm willing to bet now that Diana chose that night to make one last play for Harry. She was dressed up for something important when I saw her later. That night was the worst possible time for her to approach Harry, since I'd just confronted him with Mary's death. Harry ended up drunk on the beach, and Diana came to me to say she was giving up."

"Then I was right about her dive into the lake being a stunt," O'Malia said.

"Yes. She did it to shake me off her trail long enough for her to collect her things. Then she made her way back to Madison, hitchhiking probably, and showed up at the house she'd shared. Vicky called the police, and Diana took off, spending the night with her mother. The next day, while I was searching Madison for her, she was moving south again, back to Spring Lake. She was going to try to get her roommates' money from Harry. She saved him instead."

"Here's a coincidence I'd reject if I were reading all this in a novel," O'Malia said. "How did Diana happen to arrive on the very evening Harry Ohlman decided to kill himself?"

"She didn't, exactly. Harry told me that he's been staring at that pill bottle every night. I think he meant that he's been trying to decide night after night to take his own life. He was passed out last night when Diana arrived, unannounced as usual. She saw what Harry was up to and took the pills to save him."

O'Malia tossed what remained of her cup at a trash container. "You keep saying that Diana saved him, but I'm not buying it. She was at the end of her own rope, remember. Harry Ohlman wouldn't acknowledge her, her money was gone, her friends were going to have her arrested. She could have saved Harry by throwing the pills in the lake. Instead she swallowed them. Why couldn't she have simply been attempting suicide, like you expected her to all along? I think she

just stole Harry's way out like she stole her roommates' money.''

I was still looking for an answer to that when a
nurse appeared at the head of a hallway to our left.
She signaled to O'Malia. "The girl is awake," the
nurse said.

"Come on, gumshoe," O'Malia said to me. "This
concerns you, too. Your friend will be okay till we get
back."

Diana's bed was one of six in a large room that had
as many monitors and lights as an arcade. Only one
other bed was occupied, a fact I guessed at from the
curtains drawn tightly around it. Diana's curtains were
open, and a young man was helping her drink something. He held the cup in one hand and cradled her
head in the other.

The nurse had exaggerated when she said that Diana was awake. She was just on the verge of waking,
her dark gray eyes opening and closing repeatedly
without focusing on anything. Then they fixed on me,
and she smiled. "Hello. Clarence," she said, her voice
dry and soft.

I stepped closer and picked up her limp hand.
"You're gong to be all right," I said.

There was no answering movement from the cold
fingers. "Is Paul okay?" she asked.

"Harry's fine," I said. "You saved him."

Diana's smile slowly faded, and her eyes lost focus
in concert. "I knew you'd come," she whispered as
her eyes closed. "I said a prayer to Brigid."

I held her hand for a minute or two. Then the young
man said: "She'll be sleeping for a while. We'll keep
an eye on her."

O'Malia nodded to him and led me back out into the hallway. "What's with this Clarence business?" she asked.

"That's a nickname Diana gave me. She called it an angel name. I don't know where she got it. She kidded me about being Harry's guardian angel."

O'Malia chuckled. "Only watching movies with detectives in them has made you a cultural illiterate," she said. "Haven't you ever seen *It's a Wonderful Life?*"

"Once, I think."

"You must spend your Christmases on the moon. Clarence is a character from that movie. He's an angel." O'Malia suddenly stopped walking. Her head was bent forward, and her hands were thrust into the pockets of her suit coat. When she finally turned to me, I was surprised to see a look of wide-eyed amazement on her broad face. "Clarence saves Jimmy Stewart from suicide. He keeps Stewart from jumping into the river by jumping in himself. Then Stewart has to save Clarence. That was Diana's favorite movie, you said. Could she have had that in mind last night?"

O'Malia shook her head as though she were trying to clear it. "What am I saying? Diana must have been out to take her own life. She can't have counted on you finding her in that church, unless she thinks you really are an angel."

"It'll never be as black and white as her old movies," I said. "We may never know what Diana really intended. She may not know herself. But I'm sure she saved Harry last night. I heard it in his voice. She forced him out of himself. He still has a lot of work ahead of him, but I think he's going to make it."

We walked together as far as the waiting-room door. Harry was sitting up now, blinking at the fluorescent dawn.

O'Malia nodded toward him. "Are you going to keep an eye on him till his family shows up, or should I post a guard?"

"I'll do it," I said. "I'm still on the payroll."

She extended her hand. "Good-bye then, gumshoe. And thanks. If you ever need a license plate checked or a fingerprint traced, just dial 'O,' for O'Malia."

TWENTY-EIGHT

HARRY AND I stopped for breakfast at a café named "The Egg." Its small tables were set with bright, mismatched china, and each one had a tall carafe of ice water standing in its center. As soon as we sat down, Harry picked up our carafe and drained it to the bare cubes. Our waitress, who arrived at the end of his performance, was disconcerted.

"Another, please," I said, handing her the empty. "With a straw."

Harry ignored his menu, so I ordered for him. "I've been told that food's the best thing for a hangover," I explained afterward.

He smiled at that, unexpectedly. "I thought you were an authority on hangovers in your own right," he said.

Harry looked as bad as I'd ever seen him, with bloodshot, dark-circled eyes, a two-day beard, and scraggly hair that stuck out at odd angles like an exercise in semaphore. But it was also the best I'd seen him look since I'd arrived in Spring Lake. His slight, superior smile made him seem like the old Harry, and I grew more confident about the claim I'd made to Pat O'Malia. Diana Cory *had* saved him.

"What are you staring at?" Harry asked.

"You. You're a mess. If your eyes were any more sunken, you'd be seeing backward."

Harry's smile developed a familiar, crooked bend. "Detective talk," he said disparagingly. "Right out of a cheap paperback. I guess you're entitled, after last night. Thanks for sticking by me.''

His gratitude embarrassed me unintentionally. I wanted to tell him what a bad job I'd done of sticking by him, but he was already moving on. "I want you to do another favor for me," he said.

"What's that?"

"Hear my confession."

"You want a priest, not a second-rate bodyguard."

"How about a first-rate friend?"

"I'm not even that, Harry."

"Mary always said you were."

That beat me. Harry had cited an authority who was, for the two of us, unimpeachable. "Go ahead then," I said.

Harry's gaze dropped to the plaid tablecloth. "I met Diana Cory at an art class I was taking at Drew. It was an evening-school class, but a good one. That class and Diana were almost one and the same for me. I mean that I fell in with her for the same reasons I took the class. To meet the same needs."

It was Harry Ohlman the lawyer giving evidence before me, frowning with the effort of being clear and concise. "I wasn't happy, Owen. Looking back now, that seems incredible. If I could only be in that same rut today, going to the office I hated—Dad's office—but coming home to Mary and Amanda every night, I'd thank God on my knees. But last fall I didn't feel that way. I thought that every day was the last one I could take.

"I don't have to tell you how I've sold out since college. You remember the bragging I used to do at Boston about how I was going to stand up to Dad and be my own man. How I was going to be an artist instead of a lawyer. You know what came of that.

"I thought I'd talked myself out of caring years ago. But I was really just too busy to feel anything. After I'd taken over the firm and my days had settled into a routine, I had time to think. I realized then that the things I'd worked so hard to get weren't worth what I'd given up."

"You had Mary," I said before I'd thought better of it.

Harry looked me in the eye. "Mary was never the prize in any trade-off. She was part of my life before any of that. I think she would have preferred the painter, maybe even respected him more, but the bottom line for her was loving me. She wanted me to be happy, whatever I did. It was my job to get that done, and I screwed up.

"I was cheating the minute I signed up for that class. Not on Mary, not that quickly. I was cheating on Ohlman, Pulsifer, and Hurst, on Dad's plans for me, on what I'd become. Taking that class was like meeting an old high-school sweetheart and then seeing her on the sly. Instant old times, old ideas, old perspectives.

"Then I met Diana, and the real cheating started. You're going to hate me for this part, Owen." Harry sounded like he was looking forward to it. "Mary's love was a constant in my life, but my feelings for her changed over the past few years. They were kicked around by my sense of failure, by the idea that I was wasting my life. I told you just now that Mary was never part of my compromises. That's true, but I didn't see it that way last fall. I saw Mary and Amanda as part of the whole package, part of the firm and the house and the cars, part of the weight I had tied around my neck.''

There were tears in Harry's eyes. I held up my hand. "That's it,'' I said. "You've been through too much already. We'll talk about this later, when things have quieted down.''

"No." Harry spoke with the same authority I'd heard him use on the steps of St. Brigid's the night before. "I want to tell you. If I'd talked it out with you after the accident, none of this would have happened."

He didn't wait for me to argue the point. "When I said before that Diana and the art class were both the same for me, I meant that they were both part of the same secret revenge I was taking against my life. It sounds unbelievably stupid and shallow, but that's what it was."

Harry wiped his eyes with the back of his hand and returned to a statement of the facts. "It started with just a hello to Diana before class one night. She's remarkable, so beautiful and so unconscious of it. So unfettered in general by social bindings and rules. Totally ignorant of them, like a newborn. It makes me sound old to say it, but that part of her floored me as much almost as her beauty. It seemed wonderful after a day spent wrangling over words and forms and appearances. There was no waltzing around a subject with Diana, no rituals to observe. I was sleeping with her before I knew her last name.

"If I'd had more time to think about it, to get to know her, maybe I would have stepped back the way I always had before. That doesn't sound very fair to Diana. I don't mean it that way. She's a nice kid; I should never have used her like that."

Poor Diana, I thought. She'd been no great passion for her Prince Charming, nor was she now, after all she'd done for him. Just a good kid and an unlucky one.

"There's no point in talking about what I might have done," Harry said. "I might have broken it off. I might have told Mary everything and taken my chances. I was caught instead."

"By whom?"

"Wouldn't you like to know." A trace of Harry's crooked smile returned. "By God, fate, life. By something."

"By the accident," I said, giving the something a meaningless name.

"Yes," Harry said. "It wasn't just that I had to live my life without Mary. I had to live every day knowing what I'd done to her, with no hope of ever putting it behind me. Living on the outside always, with no way back in." His voice slowly faded and then stopped. "It's difficult to explain," he finally said.

"You can never be forgiven by Mary," I said. "She's the only one who can do it, and she's gone."

"You understand that?"

I would have happily basked in his awe and admiration at another moment. Now it seemed dishonest. "A nun explained it to me."

Harry nodded as though that made sense to him. "I remember the Sisters telling us in grammar school about sinners who had died on their way to the confessional. They made it sound as though eternal damnation was a matter of bad timing. They were right."

Our eggs arrived, now that neither of us was interested. We poked at them silently. I was trying to think of some formula of absolution that would free Harry, but I searched without hope. He had surely explored every memory of Mary's love and forgiveness without finding peace. What could I add now?

Harry seemed to be conscious of my dilemma. After the dishes had been cleared away, he said, "You haven't forgiven me yet. Isn't there supposed to be forgiveness at the end of a confession?"

"You knew Mary," I began.

"Not for her," Harry said. "Forgive me for yourself, Owen. For betraying your ideal, your first love. For trying to hurt you with that story I told you about how you'd disappointed Mary. For socking you."

"I forgive you."

Harry shook his head as he pushed his chair back from the table. "You're too easy," he said.

I thought that Harry's confession pretty much wrapped it up as far as Spring Lake and I were concerned, that I had all the answers. I was wrong. There was one more twist in store for me and one more surprise for Harry.

Harry roused himself when we pulled up in front of his cottage. "What's the program, Owen?" he asked. "Do you sit and stare at me until the men in white suits arrive? You don't have to," he added, embarrassed. "I don't have any more pills."

"Where were they, by the way? I didn't find them when I searched your cottage the other day."

"They were in my clarinet," Harry said.

"Serves me right for not being musical."

Harry's embarrassment had helped me to a decision. "I'm going to get some sleep. I think you should, too."

"Thanks," Harry said. He got out of the car and then addressed me through the open window. "If you don't mind, I think I'll take a walk first."

I waved in answer and pulled away from the curb. I drove around to the other side of the lake and turned into the first street I came to. Then I parked the Chevy in a shady spot and waited. I felt safe enough leaving Harry alone, but he was still my charge. And I was still curious.

From my seat in the shade, I watched Harry cross the footbridge. I gave him the usual head start and then followed him on foot in a reenactment of the morning ritual that now seemed so far behind us. As on those walks, Harry marched along oblivious to the world around him. There was a difference, though. He wasn't staring at this sunny morning with wide, unseeing eyes. He walked with his head down, lost in his own thoughts.

Harry led me away from the lake and up Durbin Street to the ocean. The beach gate was unattended at this early hour, and we passed through it unchallenged. I'd left my tie in the car, but that small change failed to transform my dress shirt and pants into a beach outfit. Luckily, there were few people about to stare, and the gulls took no notice of the formal tracks my oxfords left in the sand.

Harry's pace had slowed, and his head had bowed even further, his chin surely resting on his chest. I watched his shoulders for some evidence that he was crying again, but they were steady. Then slowly, Harry raised his right hand, its palm upturned and its fingers outstretched, as though he were extending it to a person walking next to him. He held his hand out through the course of three or four limping steps.

Then he stopped, and without drawing in his hand, he turned his head to examine it.

He was still standing there staring when I came up to him. "What's the matter?" I asked.

Harry seemed neither surprised nor offended to see me. "I held my hand out to Mary," he said. "It's not what you're thinking, Owen. I wasn't pretending. I was thinking of her, thinking of what I told you at the restaurant, how Mary had always supported me and how she only wanted to see me happy."

"And?"

"I was thinking about what I'd do next, whether I'd try to go back to the firm or maybe go to school again, to study and paint. And then I held out my hand." He demonstrated, holding the spread fingers of his right hand up as though he expected to receive something.

"I thought Mary was walking next to me. I felt her presence, I mean, as steady as the sun on my back. It was so real."

"You forgot for a moment," I said.

Harry considered that idea and then shook his head. "I didn't forget. I remembered. Things were quiet enough in my head for the first time in months, and I remembered something I'd lost."

"What?"

"The feeling of having her with me. I felt it again."

He was suddenly beaming at me, and I didn't like it. "Come on back now," I said.

Harry banged me on the shoulder. "I'm all right, Owen. I really am. You go back. Get some sleep. I'm going to sit here for a while."

I left him and climbed up to the boardwalk. When I looked back down, he was sitting on the sand, staring out at the ocean and other, unseen things.

TWENTY-NINE

I DIDN'T GO BACK to my rented room. Harry's pantomime on the beach had shaken me too thoroughly. I
tried to walk off the feeling of unreality, like a drunk
trying to undo a killer nightcap. I thought I was wandering aimlessly, but that would have been impossible
in Spring Lake, a town where everything led to something else. I wasn't really surprised then when I found
myself in front of St. Brigid's. I was too late for the
daily mass. The center door opened as I approached
the church, and three early worshippers emerged. One
of them was Helen Glass. She looked away when she
saw me coming up the stairs toward her. I interpreted
her sudden shyness as a lingering side effect of Pat
O'Malia's head knocking and let her pass.

Inside the church, Father Peter was soldiering on
alone. He had removed his ceremonial vestments, and
now he was extinguishing the candles on the altar, using a bell-shaped snuffer on the end of a brass rod. He
moved with surprising formality through this simple
task, holding his free hand against his stomach and
moving sideways in a measured pace along the length
of the altar. It was a drill I recognized from my days
as an altar boy.

The priest must have heard my steps on the stone
floor. He turned toward me after dealing with the last
candle. "Owen," he said. "I heard the good news
about Diana." Peter had ridden with Diana in the
ambulance, but he'd left the hospital quietly when her

condition had stabilized and Pat O'Malia had shown up. "Thank God we were in time."

"Yes," I said.

"I see you got your hand sewn up. Will there be a scar?"

"There always is." I was all but preoccupied by a strange physical phenomenon. The massive church seemed to be swaying slightly, like a rowboat tied to a dock.

Father Peter took me by the arm and sat me in one of the pews. He entered the pew in front of me and remained standing, his arms crossed on his chest. "What's the matter?" he asked.

"My hours catching up with me, I guess."

"How's Harry?"

"He's fine. I think he may have finally forgiven himself."

"You don't sound very happy about it."

I wasn't, and the realization was unpleasant. I'd grown used to feeling sorry for Harry in the months since Mary's death, after years spent envying him. Now he had suddenly leapt past me again. Harry had Mary back somehow. I didn't understand it, but I knew it was true. He had Mary again, and I was shut out.

It would have been a good moment to tell Father Peter that he'd been right all along about Mary and me, that I'd never really given her up, that my feelings for her had overshadowed every later relationship in my life and hobbled my investigation in Spring Lake. I could have tied it in neatly with my current feelings, if I could have admitted to the priest that I was jealous of a widower and his memories.

It was the moment to tell somebody all that, but I held back, as I had on the phone with Peter's secular counterpart, Edward Hennix. I changed the subject. "Don't leave Spring Lake," I said. "At least not with your tail between your legs. You didn't do anything to be ashamed of. Diana will back you up on that."

"I see," Peter said. "You think that my position has improved as a result of last night's excitement." He looked toward Brigid Kelly's alcove. "I'll be surprised if my parishioners agree with you. I'm afraid having Diana attempt suicide in their church will confirm their worst opinions of me. Even our formidable public safety director is going to have a hard time coercing them into forgiving me."

"Then you'll have to forgive them," I said.

"There are larger issues now than whether I stay in this parish or leave, Owen. I'm wrestling with questions you faced back in the seminary. Ever since I heard your history, I've judged you harshly because you gave in to your doubts. I'd like to apologize for that now. I've begun to think that of the two of us, you're the more honest man. I'm also sorry for playing amateur psychologist on the subject of you and Mary Ohlman. That was out of line. I think I was trying to hurt you when I brought that up. I was bothered by the idea of Diana turning to you for help."

"Professional jealousy," I said, volunteering the assessment I'd made at the time.

"Perhaps," Peter said. "Or perhaps there was an emotional involvement at work that I wouldn't even admit to myself. Perhaps the good people of Spring Lake have been right about me all along."

"Then you'll have to forgive yourself."

"You've got forgiveness on the brain today."

That opening was too good to pass up. I fought to rouse myself from the depths of the pew. "Forgiveness is what this case was all about. People dying for want of it. People crushed under forgiveness they never used. I spoke with a nun about it the other day. Sister Theresa. She's related to the town and to this church. She had a theory about St. Brigid's, that it's a storehouse of forgiveness. People stock it with forgiveness they can't deliver and sinners come after it because they can't live otherwise."

Father Peter looked around the darkened church. "A storehouse, did you say?" He drew his crossed arms tighter together. "That would explain the temperature. It's an interesting theory, especially coming from a religious person. A humanistic theory, wouldn't you say? Where does God come in?"

"I don't know yet."

"I like the 'yet,' Owen. I hope you work it out someday." He took my upper arms and pulled me forward out of the pew. "In the meantime, go home and sleep it off. You can't solve them all."

I DON'T REMEMBER the walk back to the Gascony and my room, but I know I made it, because I woke up in my antique bed at two o'clock that afternoon. I could have slept on until two in the morning, but the vague idea that I had pressing business nagged me upright. I was standing under my languid shower before I remembered the nature of the business. I had to go to the hospital to visit a sick friend.

The hospital where they'd taken Diana was the same one I'd visited with Father Peter the day I'd accompanied him on his rounds. I thought of that day as I crossed the brick plaza in front of the main entrance,

remembering how the priest and I had believed ourselves rivals for Diana's business and her gratitude.
Instead, we'd only been bases that she'd touched in a
game she'd been playing with Harry, a game whose
rules no one had known, least of all the players themselves.

I was still hoping for more from Diana. I must have
been, because I stopped in the hospital's gift shop to
buy her a suitor's bouquet, a twin to the one I'd taken
to the cemetery the day before. My long divorce from
Mary was final at last, it seemed, and there was a seed
of promise in that sad idea. Maybe I would move on,
now that Mary was beyond my reach forever. Maybe
it had been the memory of Mary after all and not my
endless questioning that had caused me to spend so
many of my days alone. In other words, hope was
springing, eternal and silly.

I carried other presents in addition to the flowers,
the most expensive gifts I'd ever taken to a woman.
They were a used videotape of a corny movie and a
souvenir pillow that bore the emblem of a university.
Not much to look at, but I'd paid a thousand dollars
for them. It occurred to me as I rode up in the elevator that events had legitimized the expenditure, and
Harold Ohlman, Sr., would have to eat it and like it.
I'd talk him out of the other four thousand before I
was through. Diana deserved it.

Diana's room was private through the accident of
the second bed being empty. Or perhaps it wasn't an
accident. I'd been afraid that I'd find her in a ward,
under constant observation. With no evidence to go
on, I decided that Diana's privacy was the result of Pat
O'Malia's influence.

Diana lay in the bed nearest the window, her face turned toward the light. Her skin had a milky paleness in spite of her tan, and her rebellious hair was pressed flat in odd places, as though it had been packed badly for a long trip. She was still beautiful though, even in a borrowed hospital gown that billowed about her like an extra sheet. As I watched her, I realized that the old Diana, the mysterious rich girl with her dark secrets, was gone forever. The woman before me was a stranger, regardless of all I'd learned about her past. A new mystery to be solved.

She gave a minute's free gazing and then turned her face from the light. "Hello, Clarence," she said. Her voice still had a soft edge from the pills she'd taken or some medication she'd been given.

I set the flowers down on her nightstand. "Picked these myself."

"The police lady said you saved me," Diana said. "You and Peter and..."

"Yep. All three of us." I searched for an apt reference from one of her old movies. "It was just like the end of *The Wizard of Oz*. We got the broomstick and everything."

Diana rewarded my effort with a smile. "Then I must be on the farm with Auntie Em. I'd like to be."

Her eyes were suddenly wet, and I produced her other presents with awkward haste. "I thought you might like these," I said.

I expected surprise and awe and perhaps even the suggestion that I might be an angel after all. Instead, I saw a shadow of the fear I'd produced in her the evening at her rented house when I'd asked about Paul. "You know everything then," she said.

I took her hand. "I know about the trouble in Madison. That's taken care of, or soon will be. And I know what you did for Harry. I'm proud of you."

"What I did *to* him," Diana corrected. "I ruined his life."

"No. What happened was part accident and part Harry. We carry our own messes around with us, to quote a roommate of yours. Harry shared his mess with you, that's all."

Diana turned her face toward the window. I held her hand and waited. When she turned back to me again, her eyes were dry and the fear was gone from them, replaced by something ominously like contrition.

"Sorry for using you," she said.

What was I to say to that? Something glib and detectivelike would be right, something to show that I hadn't been touched by her, that I wasn't the loser. "Any time."

I was still holding her hand. I shook it lightly as I released it. She grabbed my arm before I could move away and pulled me down gently for a good-bye kiss. "Thank you," she said.

As I CAME OUT of the hospital's revolving door, I saw Father Peter striding toward me in his unseasonable black suit. His hand touched the scar on his forehead as he greeted me. "You're looking better," he said.

"Thanks. Visiting anyone in particular?"

"A possible convert I was working on. I thought in her weakened condition I might land her."

"Good luck."

"I'm thinking things over, Owen. I'm not promising anything. I'm going to take it day to day."

"That's our motto," I said.

THIRTY

THE OHLMANS ARRIVED two days later, *en masse*. Mr. and Mrs. Ohlman's Lincoln pulled up first in front of Harry's cottage. They were not the first ones out of the car, however. That honor belonged to Amanda, who ran to Harry in a wordless demonstration of forgiveness. The Masthead Farm station wagon arrived next. It was driven by Ralph, the taciturn retainer, as I'd expected. I had not anticipated the wagon's other occupant, Ms. Kiefner, Harry's cool and efficient secretary. Ms. Kiefner had always been especially cool toward me, and the idea of reviewing my current expense report with her made my kneecaps twitch involuntarily.

The reunion on the front lawn was as warm as I could have wished. Amanda beamed, Harry and his mother teared up, and Mr. Ohlman looked on with something short of disapproval. Harry's father stole a glance at me once during the proceedings. I wasn't hoping for a show of newfound respect, so I wasn't disappointed. His expression was more like total mystification—a result, I decided, of my sketchy telephone report and his son's remarkable transformation. Harry held Amanda and hugged his parents as though their long separation had somehow been against his will. Then he led his family into the house. They were followed by two of the three Ohlman employees, all of whom had remained at a discreet distance during the hugging. The third employee, Owen Keane, turned and walked away.

I told myself that I needed a quiet moment to figure out the Whitman poem before Mrs. Ohlman asked me about it, but that was only a thin excuse. I didn't feel like celebrating. I was happy enough for Harry and Amanda, but Harry's private miracle had made the mysteries I'd solved seem inconsequential and reopened older, deeper wounds.

I sat down in the shade at the edge of the lake, which was as still as a reflecting pool, and opened *Leaves of Grass* to "Out of the Cradle Endlessly Rocking." Whitman had surely written the poem in less time than it had taken me to read it. It felt as though months had passed since the moment on the Gascony's porch when I'd decided that the poem was a mystery story. Since then, the poem had seemed a string of clues to Harry's secret, as I'd read into it my own half-realized guesses and fears. I'd been only a few lines from the poem's end and its solution at Mary's grave when Whitman's chant of "death, death, death, death" had awakened me to Harry's danger. Death was the final word, whispered to the boy/poet by the ocean, "Hissing melodious, neither like the bird nor like my arous'd child's heart." In the few lines that remained, the poet worked to "fuse" his three sources: the song of the bird, "my dusky demon and brother;" the poet's own songs, "awaked from that hour;" and "the word up from the waves,/ The word of the sweetest song and all songs," death.

I set the poem down, finished at last. If I'd read it correctly, the boy became a poet by listening to the bird's sad song and learning of death. Harry's mother had been reminded of the poem because she thought that her son was undergoing that same transformation, I now realized. She had believed that his suffering was making an artist of him in Spring Lake, when before he'd been only a talented dabbler. She'd been wrong when she'd made that guess. Harry hadn't been standing at the ocean hearing death in the fall of every wave and staring the reality of it in the face. He'd been hiding from the word in a fantasy as pretty and unreal as any of his college paintings.

Mrs. Ohlman's intuition had been wrong, but I began to feel that she might yet be right. Harry had certainly changed, almost beyond recognition, which might have explained his father's wary look at their reunion. Mr. Ohlman might have sensed that while he'd regained a son, he'd lost a lawyer forever. What Harry might become instead was an open question and a hopeful one. Any future seemed possible for him now.

Not so for me. That might have been the real cause of my depression. While Harry was standing on a new road, unburdened of his old sins, I was back where I'd begun. Less well off than I had been, in fact, because I had lost the possibility of Mary. I had lost her and Harry hadn't. I couldn't help contrasting my hopeless, self-conscious monologue at her grave with the moment on the beach when Harry had reached out, thoughtlessly and certain, for her hand.

I extended my right hand now in imitation of Harry, feeling its emptiness pass through me. That despair lasted only a second. Then I almost jumped as my hand was grasped. The hand that held mine didn't belong to a ghost. It was a real, warm, human hand and a tiny one. Amanda's.

"Snuck up on you," she said.

"Everybody does," I told her. I was about to lecture her on wandering off by herself when I noticed Ms. Kiefner standing back by the edge of the street.

"Thank you for finding Daddy," Amanda said. My client was trying to be businesslike, but her happiness was making her small face spread and dimple.

I smiled myself, struck again by Amanda's resemblance to her mother and thinking that Mary would have thanked me this same way, formally and politely, but with her joy breaking through. "You're both welcome," I said.

Amanda tugged on my sore hand until I stood up. "We're going inside now," she said.

So we did.

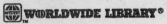

APPEARANCE OF EVIL
Carolyn Coker
An Andrea Perkins Mystery

First Time in Paperback

THE FINE ART OF MURDER

As houseguest of one of the Huntington Museum's board members, art restorer Andrea Perkins is dimly aware of the discovery of a corpse on the grounds of the museum.

LAPD detectives Roberson and Lopez, however, are very involved, exploring a connection between the dead body—and the acts of a graffiti artist who is spraying garish clothes on the statues.

But when the search for the killer begins to involve Andrea's hostess, Andrea must confront a disturbing appearance of evil that even wealth and beauty cannot hide.

"Top-notch characterization..."—*Publishers Weekly*

Available in December at your favorite retail stores.

MURDER AT THE CLASS REUNION

TRISS STEIN

A Kay Engels Mystery

First Time in Paperback

CLASS KILLER

After making it "big" as a New York journalist, Kay Engels returns to her twentieth high school reunion, hoping to find a good human interest story.

So when Terry Campbell, voted Best Looking in Her Class, is found strangled in her hotel bed while her classmates danced nearby, Kay's got her story. Terry had always been poison, and age had not impoved her.

As Kay puts her reporter's instincts into police business, she finds romance with the former class bad boy and uncovers a shocking secret in her own past. Then another murder brings her closer to a killer who will give her the story of a lifetime...but she may be too dead to write it.

Available in October at your favorite retail stores.

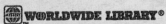

REUNION

TRAIL OF MURDER

Christine Andreae
A Lee Squires Mystery

First Time in Paperback

ROCKY MOUNTAIN MURDER

English professor Lee Squires signs on as camp cook for a wilderness outfitter hired by the wealthy and dysfunctional Strand family.

As the group begins the week-long trail ride through the Bob Marshall Wilderness, patriarch Cyrus Strand maliciously announces that he's written a new will disinheriting his spoiled and avaricious children from his immense fortune.

Suddenly, Montana's pristine beauty turns menacing as greed and rage litter the scenic expanse. And now, between whipping up elk meatballs and sourdough bread, Lee must negotiate a trail of murder that turns deadlier by the day.

"The author is remarkably sure-footed."
—*New York Times Book Review*

Available in November at your favorite retail stores.

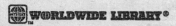

WORLDWIDE LIBRARY®

TRAIL

Nun Plussed
MONICA QUILL
QUILL

First Time in Paperback

A Sister Mary Teresa Mystery

UNHOLY ALLIANCE

Sister Mary Teresa Dempsey (Emtee), of the declining Order of Martha and Mary, follows another calling, this time to investigate the untimely death of former protégé Elizabeth Doyle.

Fatally beaten, the victim is believed to have interrupted an intruder searching for a rare thirteenth-century manuscript belonging to her estranged husband, Gregory Doyle. But when Gregory confesses to the crime, Emtee suspects that there is more afoot than mere greed.

Emtee is convinced that Gregory is innocent and hiding something. And when a second murder occurs, she discovers that the simplest of motives can be the most deadly....

"Sleuth par excellence..."
—*Los Angeles Times Book Review*

Available in December at your favorite retail stores.

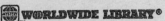

NUN